SONS OF THE WESTERN FRONTIER

VOL. II

OUTLAWS AND LEGENDS

CORGI BOOKS
TRANSWORLD PUBLISHERS LTD
A National General Company

OUTLAWS AND LEGENDS:
SONS OF THE WESTERN FRONTIER

A CORGI BOOK 552 08429 8

Originally published in Great Britain in one volume together with RED BROTHER AND WHITE under the title SONS OF THE WESTERN FRONTIER by Herbert Jenkins Ltd.

PRINTING HISTORY
Herbert Jenkins edition published 1968
Corgi edition published 1970

This book is set in 10/11 pt Times.

Corgi Books are published by Transworld Publishers Ltd., Bashley Road, London, N.W.10.
Made and printed in Great Britain by
Hunt Barnard Printing Ltd., Aylesbury, Bucks.

Contents

For
John Francis Marion
A good friend of the western
story and of mine

Sources

SONS OF THE WESTERN FRONTIER is drawn in part from the historical novels of the author. Among these works are *The Brass Command*, *From Where the Sun Now Stands*, *Death of a Legend*, *San Juan Hill* and *The Crossing*. Essentially true where they deal with actual events or persons, the stories in SONS OF THE WESTERN FRONTIER contain that amount of original and fictional material necessary to the spirit of the tale, or its accommodations of chronology. "Rough Riders of Arizona" is taken from *San Juan Hill* by Will Henry.

FOREWORD

In the many books about the Old West, too little is made of how young and how worth remembering so many of its heroes were.

Everyone has heard of Jesse James. Yet who recalls his small friends, Bud and Buck, and their fateful roles in Jesse's grim history?

How notorious the saga of Billy the Kid, who died with a man killed for every one of the twenty-one years of his violent life. Yet who recounts the strange childhood of the New York City urchin whose mother's name was Kathleen Bonney, and who himself was known from Silver City to Santa Fe as young Billy Antrim?

Benito Juarez, as every student knows, was the hero President and savior of Mexico. But who remembers the name of Chamaco Diaz, the orphaned Toltepec boy who was the savior of Benito Juarez?

There were, too, the remarkable animals whose names were so inseparably intertwined with the fates of their young rebel masters. But who today will know of Butterball? Old Hickory? La Chispa? Or El Lobo?

They are all remembered here, recorded beside the names of their unknown vanished masters. Masters whose names shared only the common bond of being young when the new land was young. Names like Pete Easter, Malquierdes Segura, Billy Hecker, Perro Dogboy, Nameless Joe, Clarence Boyd Hanks and Dingus Samuels. Young people of no fame, making no remembered mark on history, but who took their small parts bravely and with high spirit in the winning of that wild untamed frontierland which, in their memory, might well be called the Young West, rather than the Old.

VENGEANCE OF JESSE JAMES

In old Missouri the conspiracy of spring, insofar as the oldest man can remember it from the words of his grandfather, has budded in April, flowered in May.

By the final week of the latter month the dogwood and the box elder have completed their vernal agreement with the Indian pink and the mayapple. In the loamy bottomlands the bluejoint and timothy grasses have tinted every treeless acre with their waving green. And the darker cover of the hardwood forest has finished leafing out to lie in a continuous cloud, earthbound and endless in its embrace of the near and of the distant hills.

The twenty-seventh of May, 1856, was no different.

Beauty lay everywhere upon the land. The sun was in the meadow, the shadow within the forest. The dew of early morning was not yet dry upon the roadside grass, the mists of its departure still drifted thinly in the creek bottoms. The meadowlark had long been on the wing. The jay was scolding, the oriole listening, the redbird talking back. And Bob White, supremely self-satisfied upon his fence post, was ignoring them all in favor of his own shrill reassurance that the good Lord was in His fitting place and all was indeed surpassing well with the world in general and with Clay County, Missouri, in particular.

It was a sentiment most apparently not shared by the two small boys malingering in the warming dust of the crossroads. As they stared up the half-mile reach of the east road, there was little question of their expressions. But when their worried gazes topped the pin-oak knoll to rest at last upon the unpainted belfry of the Pleasant

Grove schoolhouse, the pain of the moment showed beneath their knitted brows.

The elder of the boys, a square-shouldered lad of thirteen, spat uneasily into the dust of the crossroads.

"Dingus," he said to his companion, "what you reckon has happened to Bud? I bet he's took another hiding from the old Colonel. We was to meet here before the others come along to school. We ain't going to have time, happen he don't show soon."

The smaller boy, clearly, by mark of matching upturned nose and pale blue eye, the brother of the larger, did not answer.

He was perhaps seven or eight, and small for the age; neither had he the broad-shouldered, substantial look shown by his older brother. He was thin, pale, small-boned. His blue eyes appeared weak and watery, and he blinked them with a nervous rapidity which bordered on affliction. He had an oval face, wide browed and narrow of chin, and was in all completely unimpressive. Still, there was that about him, some aura of compulsion difficult to define, which projected an impact strangely beyond that of the slight figure and pinched face. When he nodded at last, his voice was as quick as the blink of his light eyes.

"Bud will show."

It was all he said. But in his manner of saying it could be detected a certain grim reliance of self which spoke volumes—and which spoke also of the regard in which the absent member of the trio was held by the spindly Dingus.

"Well, suppose he don't?" said the other. "You reckon we'd ought to go on ahead with it?"

Dingus looked at him, eyes blinking more rapidly now. "Ma wants that colored man back. We know where he is."

Again the clipped words carried meaning and point beyond their abbreviated nature. The older boy nodded but was not convinced.

"Old Eben's a no-good worker anyways, Dingus. He ain't worth a mouthful of ashes. It ain't nowhere near like Ma couldn't buy another twice as good."

"It ain't," agreed Dingus shortly. "But he's *our* property."

"Yeah, I reckon. All the same, I'd feel a heap better if Bud would come along. It's getting late."

"You losing your sand, Buck?" There was a touch of strangely quick anger in the smaller boy's question, and, surprisingly, the older lad hastily deferred to it.

"Heck no, Dingus, it's just that them thieving Jayhawkers is sort of worked up right now. Maybe we'd ought to wait a week or so."

"We done waited three days now!" snapped Dingus. "We're going to wait any more and Old Man Pettis will have Ebe undergrounded clean to Ioway!"

"Hang it, Ding, you sure it was him? Old Man Pettis, I mean?"

"I done told you. I seen him good in the lamplight. It was him. And he was heading the bunch that hit our place. You heard him yelling the orders to the others and laughing in Ma's face when she told him Ebe was all she had left to work the place now that she's busted up with Old Simms." The reference was to their recently departed stepfather.

Buck's quick scowl agreed with the apparent hardness in his younger brother's way of saying "Old Simms."

"Yeah, I know. I *heard* him, all right, but I didn't git no chance to see him like you done."

"Ma seen him, didn't she? And she said it was him, didn't she?"

"Ma could be wrong, too. You got a bunch of riders hooting and yelling and crowding their horses all over your place and in the dark to boot, she could be wrong."

"Well, she ain't," said Dingus, his scowl as sudden as it was surly. "We're going after that pesky Ebe. You got that, Buck?"

"Ma will hide us for certain when she hears," said Buck unhappily. "She's done told you a hunnert times not to fool with her gun."

"She ain't going to hear. The gun will be back in her dresser draw' before she knows we snitched it." With the defiant words, Dingus patted the butt of the big Walker

Colt protruding from beneath his waistband. Buck looked up the road and nodded with relief.

"Well, anyways, yonder comes Bud. He'll settle it."

"Ain't nothing to settle," announced Dingus flatly.

But Buck did not hear him, or chose not to hear him, and the two stood waiting for their companion to come up. As they did, each, in his own mind, was mulling over the adventure facing them.

Seventy-eight hours earlier, John Brown had swept out of Kansas on the first of his abortive raids to free the black chattels of slave-holding western Missouri. The main force of his Red Leg and Jayhawk riders had fallen upon Clay and Jackson counties, the state's primary concentrations of Kentucky and Virginia emigrants and, accordingly, its seedbed of southern sympathy. Earlier in the year, the Dred Scott decision had fanned the bed of intersectional coals, and John Brown's raid had now burst them into flaming life. For the past three days and nights Missouri's enraged southern sons had been in the saddle. For a Kansan to be seen east of the state line was to guarantee his untimely and, in more cases than not, tortured death. For their part the fanatic abolitionists of free-state Kansas answered rifle fire with rifle fire, knife steel with knife steel. Overnight, the order of the hour became covert ambush by day, open murder by night. The farmhouses burned; the barns went up in flames. The cattle were slaughtered in their pens, the citizens in their midnight beds. It was, in the terse phraseology of the times, "hell on the border."

The small Centerville, Missouri, homestead of Buck's and Dingus' mother had been among the first struck and so had gotten off lightly. Since in its opening hours the raid had been only a makeshift expedition to seize such slaves as might be encountered on a certain few Clay and Jackson county farms known to harbor them, the boys' home had suffered only the taking-off of its one bounden black man, the presently concerned Eben.

This poor fellow, an illiterate, aging field hand, had resisted his forcible liberation with as much alarm as had the boys' mother. But these first hours had long since passed. John Brown's raid was history, and the Border War was on.

In the dark light of the moment and in the still darker light of those events certain to come in their immediate futures, it is perhaps significant to consider the fact that two small boys were determined, unaccompanied by ought else save a rusted Walker Colt and a third small boy, to cross into enemy Kansas and bring back a full-grown, lately freed Negro field hand. And it is no doubt significant, in any light, to bear in mind that it was the least of the three, the blinking-eyed, barely eight-year-old Dingus, who had originally proposed and was presently most determined to carry out the blunt scheme.

Some such thoughts of John Brown's raid, though surely not as colorfully framed, were turning in the minds of Buck and Dingus as their tardy companion padded up through the dust to join them.

Bud was outwardly cut from quite a different bolt of cloth than were either of his two friends. Where one would not have looked twice at them, he would have looked three times at Bud—then looked again.

He was a tall boy, a head taller than Buck though a full year younger. Although an adolescent will generally be a gawkish caricature of the man to come, Bud was already peculiarly handsome. He walked like a young lion—large of bone, big of paw, loose of joint, and still, to be sure, a little awkward in his growing strength, but conscious, withal, of that strength, and managing instinctively to move and speak with impressive control of it.

As he greeted his waiting companions, he demonstrated an economic fluency of address which was to distinguish him throughout life and which was to remain, to the end, almost the sole trait shared in common by him and the high-voiced Dingus. History was to make of the two boys as strange a pair of blood-loyal bedfellows as will be found in the remembered legends of the frontier. Yet, from the very onset, their characters were as divergent as were their outward forms.

Bud came up to Buck and Dingus now, grinning

broadly. He spared each of them a bobtailed nod, including both of them in his short acknowledgment.

"Let's cut," he said, suiting action to direction by starting off down the west road at a lively dogtrot. "We ain't got no more than jest time, happen we step to it."

Buck and Dingus followed him, saving their own breath for the more important matters ahead. They shortly left the road, angling down through the brush and into the bottomlands of the Little Blue. Coming out on that stream's heavily wooded course, they moved westward along its south bank, trotting in single file and as purposefully and tirelessly as three young dog foxes out on their first spring hunt.

Old Man Pettis' forty acres lay in the Big Bend bottomlands of the Missouri, a little north of the town of Wyandotte, Kansas, and east of the Big Muddy's looping juncture with the Kaw, or Kansas, River.

The confluence of the two major streams, roiling together at their eight- and nine-mile spring currents, had built up south of their joining an invisible bar of sand, arching crescent-wide from the Missouri to the Kansas shore. It was via this perilous crossing that the three boys waded and dog-paddled their way toward the western bank, shortly after midday of the twenty-seventh. To reach the river they had walked and trotted a distance of sixteen miles in five hours, thinking no more of the effort than a city boy would of his half-mile walk to the township store. Further, they displayed no fear of a river which at the point was a full six hundred yards wide and knew no peer, then or now, for treachery of shifting current and danger of hidden, down-sucking sand boil.

On the far side they crawled up into a willow thicket to pant the breath back into their lungs and, on Dingus's sober part, to examine the capping of the Walker Colt for any possible wetting. Shortly, with breath returned and the revolver passing inspection, they were once more upon their way. By one o'clock they had circled down upon the Pettis place.

Now, from the sanctuary of an adjoining cottonwood

brake they peeringly engaged in a preliminary, albeit—on the parts of Buck and Bud—somewhat faltering, reconnaissance of its corn- and melon-planted expanse.

Old Sam Pettis was a widower of known short temper and fire-eating abolitionist sentiments. Under the best of circumstances, small boys engaged in scouting his Stone Evergreen sweet corn or Rocky Ford canteloupes could anticipate no less warm a reception than that which a double-barreled ten-gauge loading of No. 6 birdshot might supply. Under other circumstances—say, for instance, those obtaining at the moment—the prospect of invading the Pettis premises was bound to assume considerably more serious proportions than had been in force back at the Pleasant Grove crossroads.

"Dadburn it, Dingus." It was the soft-voiced Bud objecting. "It ain't going to work like you first said. We done forgot about the dang dawg!"

"Yeah, Ding!" Buck's agreement was fervent. "Maybe like you say, Ebe's sure to be hid up in that smokehouse yonder. And maybe like you say, it wouldn't be no great chore to creep in and turn him loose without Old Pettis ever knows it. But, hang it, not with that cussed Redbone hound stretched out under yonder elm. Why, the minute we broke clear of the corn patch he'd have us spotted and go to baying his fool head off."

"Likely Buck's right, Dingus," added the thoughtful Bud. "Dast we risk it? What you say?"

Dingus rubbed his turned-up nose, blinked his pale eyes. "I say I didn't forget the dawg. I thought of him, first off. But Buck said he knew him. Said he'd played with him down to Market Square in Kansas City all of one Sattiday. Said he could git him to eat right out'n his hand."

"I said *likely* I could!" defended Buck. "Now I ain't so set on it. Maybe it ain't even the same dawg. That un didn't look so big and raunchy as this un. Seems I don't recollect him being so heavy ticked down the front legs, nuther. Come to think on it, I allow that other dawg was maybe a Walker or Blue Tick and not no Redbone at all. Likely Old Pettis has got hisse'f a new hound."

"Likely you're turning chicken-livered too," grunted Dingus, eyeing his older brother. "Me and Bud kin do it alone. Go on and cut for home if you're a mind to."

"Gee, I dunno, Dingus." It was Bud, not Buck, who answered him. "That Old Man Pettis he's screwier than a peach orchard boar. I wouldn't want him to take inter us in the broad daylight. Whyn't we wait for dark?"

"Cuss it all, Bud," explained Dingus impatiently, "we wait for dark they're apt to move old Ebe on us."

"By jing, I reckon you're right on that." His companion nodded. "Drat it, it does beat all how you kin think ahead on things, Dingus."

"Say," Buck broke in hopefully, "maybe they done already moved him. By cripes, Dingus, I bet they did! Why, lookit how quiet things is over yonder to that smokehouse. Shucks. There ain't bin even a fly moved since we bin here!"

"*You* lookit," gritted Dingus, jerking his thumb irritably in the direction of his advice. "Coming to flies, them ain't raisins or elderberries clustering that cussed feed pan setting on that smokehouse stoop. That there pan has bin et out of this morning, and it'll be et out of ag'in tonight. And not by no mangy Redbone hound, nuther! Our colored man is in there, you hear me, Buck?"

"Likely Dingus is right." Again it was the drawling Bud who covered for Buck's hesitation. "How you aim to git around the dawg, Ding?"

"Same way we got around the Widder Hensley's dawg on them rattlesnake melons last summer." The undersized ringleader shrugged. "I'll mosey down the front road from Wyandotte, knock on the door, and strike the old man up for a drink of water. The dawg'll commence yammering and come around in fromt the minute he hears me. Then, soon as he does, you and Buck shag in and pry Ebe out'n the smokehouse."

"Supposing Ebe puts up a fuss and don't want to come?" asked Bud.

Dingus struggled with the big Colt, working it free of his sagging waistband, and handing it to Bud.

"He won't put up no fuss," he said quietly.

Bud took the treasured weapon, holding it a little awkwardly but with patent pride. As he poked it, pirate-style in his own trousers' tops, Buck made one last feeble try.

"Say, now, what's to do happen the old man don't shell you out no drink and we done already skun in to turn Ebe loose? Old Pettis, he'll see us right off and we won't have no more chance than a Jayhawker in Jackson County."

"Cut and run." Bud shrugged, grinning quickly. "That's what Ding'll be doing. Ain't it, Ding?"

"Never you mind." The pinch-faced Dingus did not return the grin. "You git Ebe. I'll take care of Old Man Pettis. I got some idees."

Again Bud grinned. "Yeah, I bet! You allus got more idees than a Pawnee Injun's got grayback body lice. Only trouble is, sometimes them idees is jest that."

"Is jest what?" demanded his young comrade, blinking again now. Even at eight, Dingus had a limited capacity for jokes.

"Lousy," explained young Bud, the unconscious if less than accomplished humorist of the trio.

"You're real funny, ain't you?" said Dingus unsmilingly. "You take care now, you hear?"

He started off, then turned and came back. He looked at Bud a minute.

"Maybe you'd best give the gun to Buck," he told him.

"Aw, c'mon, Ding!" Bud was at once serious. "Leave me keep the gun. I ain't never toted it, and both you and Buck has!"

"Give it to Buck," repeated Dingus. "I ain't funning with you, Bud. I don't cotton to you when you're thinking everything is so blamed funny. It'd be purely like you to up and shoot our cussed colored man."

"Aw, for cripes sake, Dingus, I ain't going to shoot pore old Ebe. What's eating you? Cain't you take nothing in fun? Leave me carry the gun now."

"Give it to Buck."

Bud looked down on the smaller lad. He towered over him. He would have made two of him with enough left over for a fair start toward a third. But in the end he grinned again and handed the gun to Buck.

"Now careful, Buck," he instructed him soberly. "Don't

shoot old Ebe, whatever you do. Not lest he starts laughing."

Buck took the weapon, not daring to return the open grin which came with it and not feeling too much like returning it, either. He watched Dingus dart down the near edge of the cornfield, then around the melon patch and along the fence rail bordering it.

Bud quit grinning and joined him in the watching. Presently they saw Dingus, smaller than ever now with the three-quarter-mile distance, pop out beyond the hedge-orange trees lining the Wyandotte Road and start down it toward Old Man Pettis' front gate. Even from the distance his cheery whistle, compounded by the carefree swing of the willow switch he had picked up en route to the road, carried clearly to them.

Bud watched the small figure for a moment more, then shook his head. "Only blamed time he's happy," he said slowly, "is when he's up to some particular hell-raising."

"He ain't bin no different since he could walk," agreed Buck frowningly. "And he could walk since he was some short of a yearling."

Dingus came abreast of the fence fronting Old Man Pettis' yard, still whistling for all he was worth. It was not enough. The sleeping hound back by the smokehouse did not miss a snore. The old widower's cabin stood silent.

Scowling, Dingus thrust the willow stick into the pickets of the fence and ratcheted it along the poles from the corner of the property to the front gate. Still no response. Unlatching the gate, he stepped through it and slammed it noisily behind him. The hound snored on. The house remained still.

He hitched up his galluses, spat into the dust of the yard, actually grinned. Starting for the front stoop, his whistle and willow switch were again going full blast.

The change in the boy's attitude since leaving his companions was little short of remarkable. He could not have presented a more appealing picture of the wide-eyed, wandering, barefoot boy. The nervous blink of his eyes, accented when he was angered or upset, was entirely gone. The thin face, normally about as pleasant as that of a weanling ferret, was beaming beneath a bucktoothed smile that would have disintegrated the heart of a limestone headmarker. When his reaching foot struck the first plank of the weathered stoop, his high-pitched "Hello in there, anybody to home?" sang out with an innocence and purity equal to any choirboy's Sunday-morning assault on "Rock of Ages Cleft for Me," or "Onward, Christian Soldiers."

The opening note of his Centerville soprano got things off to a flying start. As Bud was later to proudly recount it for the envious ears of the Pleasant Grove Class of '56, "First off, everything went slicker than the insides of peeled elm bark!"

The Redbone hound missed a snore, pulled his head up, and cleared the dust and the crawling flies from around his nostrils with a suspicious "woof!" He sat up, lifted his heavy muzzle with conscious effort, and began dutifully to bay. Presently he got up, stretched, yawned, sat back down to scratch, got up again, started trotting around the house. He had not gone ten feet before it was necessary to stop, sit down, scratch again.

On the front stoop Dingus waited, hearing the stir of the old man moving inside the house. Shortly, he came out, listened to Dingus' polite "Please, sir, kin I have a drink of your well?" and stared at the boy a moment.

"It's right in front of you, boy. Ain't nobody stopping you that I kin see. He'p yourse'f."

Dingus looked innocently at the well. It stood in the geometrical center of the front yard and he had had to walk clean around it to get to the house.

"Oh," he said diffidently, "you mean that well, sir?"

Old Man Pettis looked at him again. He sat down on the stoop.

"Well, now, boy"—he nodded speculatively—"you suit yourse'f. There's another well back yonder by the smokehouse. Then half a mile up the road there's two more at Jake Russell's place. You want to head back the way you come, you'll soon enough come to two whole rivers plumb full of the stuff. What you up to, boy? You don't look stupid to me."

"Well, I guess I ain't real bright," answered Dingus, tugging at his forelock and toeing the dust of the yard.

"Leastways, Ma allus said I ain't. Oh, please sir, could you put that dawg up?"

The ancient Redbone had shuffled around the corner of the house and leaned against the outer support of the porch roof to rest up from his long journey around from the back yard. Regaining his breath, he woofed twice, halfheartedly, at the visiting ragamuffin. Then he collapsed back into the dirt and crawled under the porch with a grateful sigh.

"Old Hickory won't bother you none," said Pettis. "He ain't got but only four teeth left in his head. He's half blind and he cain't hear a shotgun six feet away from him: happen the wind's wrong, he cain't. Only thing he's got left that's any account is his nose."

"Oh, thank you, sir! I was bit by a Redbone once. They're powerful biters. My, ain't he a grand dawg though? And see how he minds you! I sure am beholden to you, Mr. Pettis!"

Dingus' gratitude was not alone well done but a little overdone. Old Sam Pettis' eyes narrowed.

"How come you to know my name, young un?"

Dingus cussed himself. By cripes, along about now a boy better watch himself. This old coot was pretty cagey. He had let that name of his just slip out. He sure should not have let it, either. If he wasn't tolerable cautious, Old Pettis would be on to him before Bud and Buck could get Ebe out of that smokehouse and safe away across the cornfield.

He covered the slip as best he could, working his wan smile and diffident nod polite as pie.

"Shucks, sir," he stammered deliberately, "everybody knows Old M—everybody knows Mr. Sam Pettis. My ma, she pointed you out to me one Sattiday down to Market Square in Kansas City. Said what a fine figure of a man you was, and all such like as that."

The smile and the flattery began to work on the old man, but native suspicion ran strong along the border and Sam Pettis had his fair share of it. "Who's your ma?" he asked quietly, and eyed Dingus way too close for comfort when he said it.

"The Widder Hanks, over to Wyandotte," Dingus lied glibly. "I'm her second boy, Clarence Boyd."

"Well, now, that's right funny," mused his listener. "I was jest thinking I'd seen you some place else . . . like maybe over to the Simms place."

Dingus did not like the look that was getting into the old man's eye, nor the way he was standing up and watching him.

"Oh, no, sir. I don't even know the Simmses. They from Wyandotte, sir? Must be new folks, huh?"

"Well no, now, boy, they ain't." The old man was easing down off the stoop, not looking at Dingus but not fooling him any either. "They ain't new and they ain't from Wyandotte. Mrs. Simms, she's a southern lady. Got two boys from her first husband. That's the one what run off from her before she took up with Will Simms. Fergit the first husband's name, right off. Seems like he was a Baptist preacher or some such. Anyhow, that second boy, now, he looks a powerful lot like you. Only maybe not so polite and smart. Come along here, boy, let's have a look at you."

He moved toward Dingus with the command, what was supposed to be a fetching smile uncovering his few teeth. His small guest was not in the market for any fetching smiles. He backed away a little faster than somewhat.

"Oh, *them* Simmses!" He announced it as though a great white light had just broken refreshingly upon him. "Why, law now, sir, they're kin of ours, sure enough. Second cousins on my paw's side. They're bushwhackers, you're sure right there. Ma, she ain't got no earthly use for them, you kin lay!"

He was getting set to cut and run, figuring Buck and Bud had lost their nerve and never even started in for the smokehouse. And he was beginning to blink again. He would fix them when he caught up to them, by cripes. But right now he had best fix himself, before Old Man Pettis did it for him. He had backed and grinned his way clear of the corner of the house when, just before he reckoned to take off, he threw a quick look toward the smokehouse. As he did, business picked up all around.

"What in tarnal sin was that!"

Old Man Pettis stood stock-still, his jutting whiskers whipping toward the rasping sound which had interrupted the retreat of the barefoot lad before him.

Dingus could have named the noise for him, and in complete detail. He could, even had he not just seen it made with his own two eyes.

You take a stout crowbar with two husky farm lads on the prying end of it. You insert its free end under the hasp of a rusted smokehouse door. Then you have those two young ones heave down on their end of it with all their might and main. Along about that time you've got a pretty good sound of splitting door planks and squealing tenpenny nails.

His certain knowledge of the nature of the noise to the contrary, young Dingus held both his peace and his ground.

But not for long.

He held them only for the wisp of time necessary for Old Man Pettis to gallop around the house corner, and for him to stick a grubby bare foot between the bearded widower's boots, tripping him flat, and then for the old man to get his face up out of the dirt and fasten his squinty eyes on what was disappearing in a cloud of May dust across the sprouting furrows of his cornfield.

What was disappearing across those burgeoning furrows was, in the order of its wing-footed flight, an informal group of four principal items. Item one: an ancient, just reliberated Negro field hand. Item two: a short, squarely built Clay County lad of thirteen. Item three: a tall, broad-shouldered Clay County lad of twelve. Item four: a long-barreled cap-and-ball Walker Colt revolver.

The last item had somehow managed to change hands since Dingus last saw it and was now back in the prideful possession of the whooping hollering Bud. Its present four or five enthusiastic discharges into the Kansas air were doing nothing to dull the uproar of the moment.

As a matter of fact, the booming black-powder explosions were loud enough to raise the dead—or the almost dead. Old Hickory, the Redbone hound, came stumbling out from under the porch, shaking his head and baying distractedly.

Subsequent to the old hound's confused reappearance, two more flights were added to that of Bud and Buck and the reclaimed Eben. Old Man Pettis scrambled up and dove for his front door and the double-barreled ten-gauge hanging over the fieldstone fireplace; Dingus cleared the picket fence and took off up the Wyandotte Road in one and the same burst of barefoot heels.

Old Hickory ran three times around in a circle, blundered out the front gate, peered up the road with his rheumy eyes, bayed once after the fleeing Dingus, galloped back into the yard, ran gallantly into the corner support of the porch, fell down, got up, shook himself, dropped resignedly to his haunches, and began scratching again.

His hind foot was still digging apathetically at its favorite bare spot, under his right elbow, when his enraged owner came racing back out of the house with the shotgun.

Minutes later, Old Hickory was displaying his sole remaining talent.

Cursed on by his fuming master, he quartered briefly around the smokehouse, cut the barefoot tracks of the Negro slave and his dashing Clay County rescuers, and took off, baying eagerly, across the still settling dust of the cornfield. Once on the track, the old dog never faltered. He drove steadily forward, big head down, pendulous ears trailing in the dirt. At regular fifty-foot intervals he belled sonorously, not bothering to lift his muzzle from the warming scent to do so.

As Old Sam Pettis had said, Old Hickory still had a nose. And as the fleeing boys were shortly to discover, he could still use it.

Dingus, circling far east of the cornfield, saw the old man and the hound move across the mounded rows of the corn patch. The bawling notes of the old dog's voice came clearly to him. He saw, too, the bounce of the May sun off the twin barrels of the ten-gauge. Somewhere ahead, Bud and Buck and Ebe were already lost in the welcome tangle of the bottom willows, but no boy born of hound-dog country needed to be told that given time—and not much time—Old Pettis and the Redbone would come up to them. Nor did he need to be told what might happen then. It was a day and time wherein if a boy would undertake a man's work he could expect to be paid off at a man's wage.

He, himself, could cut and run. The hound was not running his track. But that was not the plan, and when Dingus made a plan nobody, not him nor anybody else, fooled around with that plan. He had said they would join up at the slough north of Old Pettis' place, and that is what they would do. Dingus would be there, and the others had best be there too.

They were.

When Dingus popped out of the brush, scratched and torn and flushed with panting, he found them waiting for him. And even as they talked, the belling of the old Redbone drew nearer and nearer.

"Now what the heck we going to do, Ding?" Buck, as usual was silent, Bud doing the asking. "We dassn't stick here and we dassn't cut and run. Ebe's turned his cussed ankle and can't do no more than limp along. That dad-blamed hound will be up to us in five minutes, and Old Pettis not more than five more minutes behind him."

"We got to do suthin'," said Buck suddenly. "We cain't jest covey up here. I reckon we've got to take a set at splitting up. That hound cain't run three ways at once, and we kin leave Ebe right here. The hound will hold up once he's come up to Ebe, I allow."

"You're allus doing a power of allowing." Dingus nodded sourly at him. "We come to fetch Ebe home, and we done got him half fetched. We sure ain't leaving him here, nuther, you hear me?"

"Blame it all, Ding, Buck's right. We got to do suthin', and right soon."

Bud was not frightened and not flustered. He was just asking for a clarification and/or change of plan. He got both, and without the least hesitation, from the blinking Dingus.

"We ain't got a blessed thing to fret about excepting

that ganted-up old hound. First thing we do is take care of him. He's a quarter mile up on Old Pettis, so we'll just leave him come along up to us."

"Now, you all do that, Mister Ding!" Old Eben, torn between old family loyalties and as yet untried freedoms, made the suggestion excitedly. "You just leave that wuthless houn' dawg come up. I'll hunker right hyar and I won't move a peg, you'll see. When he come a-puffing and a-baying along, I'll latch onto him and hold him right hyar till you and Mister Buck and Mister Bud has done scattered clean across the river. Now you lemme do that for you, Mister Ding!"

"Sure," urged Buck hopefully. "Ebe knows the old dawg, and we don't. Dawg won't give him no hard times. Ebe kin hold him here, like he says."

"Sure," mimicked Dingus, with the quick belligerency of the smaller brother. "And suppose, once we've lit out for the river, Ebe don't choose to hold him?"

The other two boys frowned at the thought, and Dingus swept on.

"No, sir, we got to take care of the dawg ourse'fs. That way we know it's did. *Then* we kin skin for the river, fetching Ebe with us. What the tarnal sin you think we come to Kansas for, anyhow?"

"Mister Ding, you trust me to hold thet houn' dawg. Leave me stay hyar in Kansas, that's all right. You run on, boy, and get free. I'll keep the dawg from follering you."

Dingus did not answer him. Instead he seized the big Walker Colt from Bud's waistband and jammed its muzzle into the pleading freedman's face. Old Eben began to weep.

"Now, Ebe," advised the blinking-eyed boy, "you jest keep up that blubbering and I'll blow your head right square off'n your shoulders, you hear?"

"Lawd help us," muttered the weary Negro, "please don't leave him do it, Mister Bud. He don't know what he's saying."

Bud nodded soberly and started to step toward Dingus. The smaller lad whirled on him, face flushed.

"Now don't *you* give me no grief, Bud!" he warned. "I

wasn't going to harm the old ninny none." With that assurance, he shoved the big revolver back into his own waistband and waved toward the river-bottom brush. "Yonder comes the dawg. How would you say to handle him?"

Bud grinned, relieved. "Why," he said, "ain't nothing to it. I got this here coil of rope I brung along to hold up my pants happen the horse-blanket pin breaks. We jest rope the old dawg to yonder cottonwood and skin for the river free as naked jays."

"That shines," agreed Buck, nervous now as the baying of the old hound sounded panting-close. "Or we kin jest rope him and tow him along with us. He ain't going to give tongue providing we're *leading* him."

"No, that won't do," said Bud. "But we could bind his muzzle shut with a piece of tore shirttail when we tie him up. Thataway, Old Pettis couldn't tune in on him for location. Time he tromps him out, we could be home and dried off. What you think, Dingus?"

Dingus shook his head. "That old rope's rotten as stump punk. Old dawg might bust it. Or suthin'."

Next moment Old Hickory had come up to them, halting the debate. He stopped twenty feet away and bawled four times lustily, letting Old Pettis know he had the game treed. Then he planted bony rear to bottom loam and began to scratch. His job was done.

Bud moved toward him, gave a low whistle, and clapped his hands. Old Hickory looked up at him and stopped scratching. Presently his tail began to club the ground in slow friendship. He got up and met the advancing boy halfway, tail still waving slowly.

Bud slipped the rope around his neck and led him uncomplainingly down toward the slough and the cottonwood-brush clump. Dingus followed him, and behind them came Buck, helping the limping Eben down the steep bank. They could hear Old Pettis thrashing through the willows above them, cussing and hollering up his missing dog with every step.

Old Hickory lifted his head to answer him, and Bud cuffed him alongside the muzzle. "Here, you, none of that now. You jest hold still till we git you trussed up here. Then you kin try and yammer all you dang please."

He turned to the silently watching Dingus.

"Here, Ding, gimme a hand. I got the old fool tied. Now all we got to do is take and halter him with our nose wrap. We'd best tear *your* shirt, though. Mine's brand-spanking new, and my daddy will hide me proper, happen I rip it up any."

Dingus moved forward, nodding. "You got him tied good and short?" he asked quietly.

"Shucks, he couldn't scrootch around enough to fetch hisse'f a fleabite." Bud grinned. "Gimme that there piece of your shirttail to bind his jaws shut."

But Dingus shook his head. "Git out'n the way, Bud," he ordered.

The other boy moved obediently aside. As he did, Dingus stepped past him toward the old dog. Bud's mouth dropped. "Here!" he cried in alarm. "You cain't do thet, Ding! Not with him tied and helpless."

"Shut up," said Dingus coldly, and taking the big Walker Colt he put it to Old Hickory's head and pulled the trigger. In the stunned silence, the ancient weapon misfired. The metallic clink of the hammer on the defective cartridge seemed to release the rawboned Bud. He leaped at Dingus just as the smaller boy pulled the trigger again. This time the revolver fired, but Bud struck Dingus' hand just as it did, and the bullet flew harmlessly over Old Hickory's head to ricochet off through the woods. Before Dingus could react, Bud seized the gun and wrested it from him. The two boys stood face to face, breathing hard.

Dingus was furious. His blue eyes blinked so rapidly they watered as if with tears. He seemed in danger of suffocating on his rage.

Bud was white as a bedsheet, but not with anger. Bud was ill. The leader, old Ding, he would have killed that poor old dog in cold blood. Indeed, he had tried to do it. Bud couldn't believe it. He felt as though he would like to go off into the trees and be sick. Instead, he turned the big Colt revolver on Dingus and spoke quick and quiet to him.

"Ding," he said, "you take Buck and Ebe and you git out'n here. Leave me and the dawg be. . . ."

He suspended the order in his soft way, but Dingus did not argue it. Cursing Bud with an oath too ugly for a boy so young, he turned and ran for the river. He said no word, gave no glance, to his brother Buck nor to the old colored man they had set out so boldly to rescue from vile freedom. Unbidden, Buck and Eben fled after him, however, for they had heard Bud's command and believed that the big-knuckled youth meant it. As for Bud, left with the Redbone hound, time was passing scant. The crashes and cries of Old Pettis were but yards away.

"Friend dawg," the boy said, cutting the animal loose, "I wisht the both of us had more brains. Good-by, and don't feel beholden to foller me."

With the words, the youth dropped the cut rope and ran down the slough bank away from the direction taken by Buck and Ebe and Dingus. Old Pettis, breaking through the scrub, saw the lad's shirttails disappearing in the far willows and loosed both barrels on the fly. But somehow Old Hickory managed to get underfoot in the final instant, and Sam Pettis stumbled over his own dog, and the screaming buckshot went high and wide of the target. It only pattered about the fugitive like softly falling rain, and Bud was lost and safe in the deeper growth before the last pellet hit the ground.

As for Old Hickory, he did not utter another bay once the boy had slashed him free of the stump. Not only did he refuse to run or cry the track, he simply slunk away and left Old Pettis blistering the bottom brush with profane vows of dire punishment awaiting the dog at the home place.

But Old Hickory, if slow, was not dense. He never went near the Sam Pettis place again. Rather, once free of Old Sam's view, he circled around and struck the track line of the Missouri boy far down the slough bank, following it out as swiftly as his stiffening bones would permit. Thus it was that, when Bud had stripped at the bank of the big river and tied his clothes in a hank to dangle from his neck and was just wading in to begin breasting the current, he heard an eager whine and an immediate large splash behind him. It was Old Hickory, of course, treading the muddy tide bravely out to join the boy who had stayed with him when it counted.

If the two found a good life after that, the legend does not say. For Bud was not a talker, nor did he leave these memoirs written down.

But the hand of another did put this beginning of the border fable in ink, within the record, and with the entry left first evidence of the violent lives to come.

Mr. Cheaver Peabody was the headmaster of the Pleasant Grove School. Upon the day in question, that long-ago and lazy springtime in old Clay County, he closed the schoolhouse after classes with a sigh of meaningful relief. Any day that young Bud and the brothers Buck and Dingus played hookey was like unto a reprieve from the gallows. Gratefully, the headmaster went to his desk, opened the attendance book, took up his quill pen.

Ah! he thought, what's in a name? These three names he was about to write down, for instance: such decent, proper names they were; downright substantial, too, and with the unquestioned ring of quality folk to them.

Yet as he entered them into the absent column, Mr. Peabody knew—he even muttered aloud to the dusty silence of the schoolroom—that these three names were destined for no good end.

"Nits make lice," he said, and scratched the three names down:

"Younger, Thomas Coleman; James, Alexander Franklin; James, Jesse Woodson."

ROUGH RIDERS OF ARIZONA

Prescott had not come on any vast amount, Pete decided, since he had last won the bareback money there three years ago in the summer of '96. The saloons still began just beyond the stage office at Gurley and Mount Vernon and ran from there on.

Pete had heard it stoutly maintained that there were other enterprises than gila juice mills in Prescott, but he questioned the idea severely. More whisky to his certain knowledge was drunk annually in that town than in the rest of Arizona Territory. They used it to chase their water with. Of course, to be fair, there was more whisky than water available. It was truly that dry in Prescott. There was naught save gray granite, white rock dust, and red-bark bull pines growing there. The creek was said to be damp for a part of certain years, but mostly it ran to ragweed, rusty cans, chicken-dusting puddles, and old bedsprings. It was needful, the natives said, to take on a quantity of liquid so as not to dehydrate and die of thirst right there among their neighbors. So they took no chances on such a terrible end.

Pete clucked to his pony. The wiry runt had recognized the town and had slowed down and tried to turn off into the Black Canyon road, toward Phoenix and Tucson. At least down that way there were the Salt and the San Pedro rivers. With a camp shovel and a little digging you could bore out a water hole even in August. But here in Prescott you took the native drink or none at all. And the little *grulla* mustang shared his rider's distaste for bottled or barreled restorants.

Ahead, now, coming into the main road from the

Black Canyon direction, was another horseman. He, too, was dust-clad from hard travel. He carried two blankets rolled behind his saddle and was young and lean and from a long ways off, just like Pete. Pete's mustang raised its head and flagged its ragged ears toward the newcomers. The other mount responded with a friendly whistle-whicker of the kind peculiar to *mesteños verdados*, be they Pecos, Panhandle, or Yavapai bred. The horses now having announced their desert kinship, it remained for the riders to do likewise.

Pete slowed his mount, watching the other youth warily. After all, even within sight of the lights of Prescott, it was still a lonely country, one wherein the travelers of merging trails did well to keep an eye on one another's attitudes.

But the stranger from the south was as hungry for a friendly word as ever Pete Easter.

He, too, pulled in his mustang and came up to the meeting, watchful and on the *qui vive*, while still getting ready to grin at the drop of a halfway well-meant hello.

"Howdy," said Pete. "Going to Prescott? I'm Pete Easter."

The other youth's narrowed eyes opened wide.

"*Big* Pete Easter?" he asked, patently floored.

Aha! thought Pete. Here is a man who has ridden a few trails. He knows what counts.

"Yep," he admitted, not even blushingly. "That's me. How come you to realize it?"

"Well," said the other, smiling in a fetchingly diffident manner, "first place, you ain't small."

Pete knew what size he was: six four and something to spare, with bones and muscles and gristle to match. He nodded a little curtly. Was this boy trying to stretch him on the fence to dry?

"Yeah," he said. "What else?"

"I seen you take the bareback money three years ago, Fourth of July," answered the slight, shy rider. "Man, you was grand."

Pete swelled to at least six five. "Thanks," he accepted graciously. "Who'd you say you was?"

"Hecker," answered the other youth quietly. "Billy Hecker, of Sonoita."

Pete let out his breath like a stepped-on toad. *"Billy Hecker of Sonoita?"* he repeated, awe-stricken.

"Yes, sir," said his companion, "the same."

Pete turned red; then white; then settled on a sort of sick medium-gray-green.

Billy Hecker of Sonoita was only the greatest saddle-bronc rider in the Southwest, barring only maybe Tom Darnell of Deming or A. R. Perry of Phoenix. And, compared to bareback, saddle-bronc riding was the fancy frosting over the plain cake. Bareback just wasn't in it with saddle-bronc. It was like salt sow to roast sirloin, or blue John milk to Jersey cream.

"Cripes!" managed Big Pete, at inspired last. "Let's ride."

In Prescott, they put up their horses at the livery stable of the stage line. Billy was overwhelmed with the grandeur of everything so far. When he had come to ride in the rodeo that three-years-gone Fourth of July, he had not stayed in town after dark. He had never seen a settlement bigger than Sonoita with its lights turned on all at once, and he could not adjust readily to such unadulterated splendor as the Hub of Yavapai County after midnight.

Moreover, in the previous visit, he had been called on to accept just the normal holiday rodeo crowd in from the surrounding range country. Now, with Teddy Roosevelt having called for volunteers to join up in his private cavalry and go to whip the vile Spaniards in Cuba, why, heck, everybody in Arizona Territory that was anybody, and hale, was in Prescott waiting for the enlistments to start out at nearby Fort Whipple. There must be, Pete and Billy estimated, just by glancing up Gurley toward the Square, close to 500 men milling around the plaza, yonder. And, by God, here it was coming up 3:00 A.M. in the morning!

Well, no wonder, thought Pete Easter, that a simple country kid like Billy Hecker was somewhat spooked by it all. It was a good thing he had an experienced guide with him, or he might have been stampeded "entire." As for Billy, he seemed to accept his debt.

"Say, Pete," murmured the Sonoita boy, as they now came out of the stage-line office, "just lookit the length of that brand on this here livery stable."

Condescendingly, Pete glanced at the sign.

It was, in truth, a beauty. THE VERDE VALLEY & MOGOLLON RIM, NORTH PHOENIX, BUMBLE BEE, OAK CREEK, COCONINO COUNTY & SOUTH FLAGSTAFF STAGE LINE & LIVERY COMPANY was not, for a fact, the sort of business title to be ignored.

Well, shucks, this was Prescott.

A man had to be ready for such sights. Big city, big signs; that was all. But then, this Sonoita kid, famous bronc rider or not, was a real greenhorn: a hick. He wasn't to be blamed.

"Come on," said Pete Easter, gesturing toward the bracelet of lights encircling the plaza, "let's us go and scout the enemy."

Billy Hecker held back some. He hadn't much money, he said. As a matter of fact, he didn't have two thin dimes to rub together. Moreover, he was not a drinking man. His tastes ran more to horse liniment for horses. To this, Pete agreed.

"Sure, Billy"—he shrugged—"me likewise. Whisky and me got no mutuality whatsoever. But, man, you got to see Prescott with the lights turned on. It's somewhat. Come on along. I got money."

"By George!" The other nodded. "I'll just go with you, Pete. It surely is fine of you to take me."

Flattered, Pete led the way.

But without bourbon the tour turned shaky. It was, after all, 3:00 A.M. in the morning. At the 5,600-foot altitude the air cut like an Apache scalp-ax. When, after a turn of the sights along Whisky Row and Tomcat Alley, with detours to see the old log Governor's mansion and the new all-stone courthouse, the wind began to rise and to whip the two young cowboys about the ears and to snap and rattle their horsehide vests like tissue paper, Pete and Billy decided they had had enough fun for one night.

Accordingly, Pete, the cosmopolite, suggested they seek out a suitable hostelry and bed down in style.

Billy demurred, reminding his new friend that he had only eight cents to last him until Teddy Roosevelt and the U.S. Army took over his keep tomorrow, or whenever. Pete patted him on the shoulder and said the pleasure would be his. After some soul-searching, the Sonoita boy agreed on the basis of considering the needed amount a cash loan to be repaid out of his cavalry salary. This arrangement "shook on," the two paladins angled across the plaza, taking more or less dead aim on an inn they had previously been impressed by. Not even Pete could recall, right off, another lobby in his enviable urban experience with such a rainbow of red leather armchairs, living green palm trees, and polished-bright brass spittoons. And, indeed, the Yavapai House was an imposing edifice—so much so, in directly upcoming fact, that when the two cowboys drew near to it, the younger lost his nerve.

"Pete," said Billy Hecker, "I got to tell you something; I ain't never been in no hotel in my lifetime."

Pete shrugged reassuringly, comfortingly. "Shucks," he drawled, "that's all right, Billy. I been in two of them."

Billy Hecker nodded, not convinced. "I dunno," he said. "Lookit that cussed whirlygig doorway."

Pete threw a superior glance at the revolving glass entryway, the only one of its kind between Kansas City and San Francisco.

"Pah, that's nothing," he said. "All the best places got them sort of gates nowadays. Come on."

He started into the door, unafraid, and Billy, gritting his teeth, stepped into the following quadrant as it came spinning around. Once inside, however, he broke and ran. Pete, taken by surprise and from the rear, was helpless. He and his comrade went whizzing around, crazy as squirrels in a cage.

Pete tried yelling and fanning with his hat to slow Billy down, but Billy had the bit in his teeth and would not be headed.

Once Pete tried leaping out of the door, to save himself, but nearly lost his nose and one ear in the attempt.

After that, he gave up and just kept running for his life. He was saved by a kindly old gentleman resident who got up from his snooze in one of the lobby chairs, limped over to the spinning door, stuck his cane into it, and brought it to a jarring halt.

Pete helped the dizzy Billy out of his section, thanked their benefactor, started for the desk. The night clerk, unamused by cowhands playing in his glass door at a quarter of four in the morning, told them that if they turned about and departed in comparative peace he would not press charges. But Pete pacified him by getting a rolled-up brown-paper sack out of his shirt front and showing him its contents—three $5 bills, a toothbrush, straight razor, picture of his mother, and 63¢ in small money. The fellow not only quieted down but rented them the primest room in the house. He said it was the Left Wing of the Presidential Suite, and he only charged them $7.50 for it.

Upstairs, they were much taken by the radish-pink, turquoise, and purple tulips of the carpet in the hallway, and also by the verdigrised brass Rochester lamps screwed right into the walls. True, there was a dismal fragrance of some order, rather like sheep-dip or ring-worm carbolic, but Pete believed that it was from the paste used for the gold and fuchsia wallpaper and claimed that it was a special imported "old-country" kind containing secret Egyptian ingredients which slowed down the vermin of one class and another and was used in all top-grade houses such as the Yavapai.

Billy nodded and said, "If you say so, Pete," then added admiringly, "Lord, Lordy, seven dollars and fifty cents just for a place to bunk one night! My goodness, think of it! And you stood to it like Old Steamboat holding still for the bucking-strap. Jings, Pete! You got more innards than a scrub bull."

Pete, still trying to recover from the trauma of letting loose of $7.50 all in one piece, shrugged weakly. "It don't take nerve once you know how," he said.

"Man!" Billy beamed, uncooled. "Seven dollars and four bits, just like that! Wow-eee!"

They let themselves into the room and turned up the bedside lamp. The odor inside was heroic.

"It'll clear up soon as we pry open the winder," declared Pete.

Billy coughed and nodded, "That must be top-quality paste, all right. It's a wonder it don't raise a blister on them walls. My, but it is stout!"

Pete muttered something general in return and headed for the window. When he had pulled it wide, a blank look came over his face.

"Billy," he said, "This here ain't no winder."

"What on earth you saying?" asked his companion. "You must be mistook. If that ain't a winder, what's outside them oilcloth draperies?"

"It's a solid brick wall," said Pete. "They done set the winder frame smack against the building next door."

"By gum, Pete, we got to have air!" Billy's voice held a note of returning panic, and Pete tried gentling him quickly.

"Heck," he said, "we'll just prop open the outside door with this here chair and draw oxygen from the hall. There, that ought to do it. Come on, now, let's hit the hay."

Warily, they got out of their pants, shirts, boots. They left their socks and hats on. The bed was skimpy and of hilly terrain. Billy surveyed it, backing uncertainly and pawing the board floor.

"That mattress," he declared, "is outer of order than the molars on a wapple-jawed mule. She is leppy looking as a crock of Grandmaw's clabber."

"Naw, no such thing!" insisted Pete, feeling the landscape of striped canvas. "She's just full of goose feathers and duck fuzz, like all them high-grade ticks. Come on, pile in, partner."

He boarded the bedstead gingerly, fearlessly pioneering the way. But Billy remained standing in his drawers alongside the foot of it. He looked a good bet to bolt again, so Pete collared him with a yell before he could.

"Cuss it," he exploded, "get in here! Ain't I told you she's safe? What I got to do? Sign you a deed?"

Billy stood on one foot, cramping the toes of the other

around his bony ankle. "It ain't that," he murmured, blushing. "It's that I ain't never slept with nobody afore now."

Pete sat up, staring at him incredulously. "Well, for Christmas sake!" he blurted. "It ain't like we was married, you know. Heck, I ain't never slept with nobody afore, neither, and I'm twenty-two years old! Now you pile in here and lemme cinch up this slinchy blanket. The draft's blowing up my drop seat fit to pull off the buttons and flap me raw."

Billy blushed again but crawled in. He lay as far over on his side as he could without falling out on the floor.

"Douse the glim," ordered Pete. "She's over on your side."

Billy reached obediently for the table lamp. When the room was dark there was a finely strained silence of some three minutes. Then Pete yelled and leaped bolt upright. Billy, inquiring as to his problem, was next instant giving a holler of his own. Scrambling wildly out of bed, he fell over the chair propping open the hall door. This melee managed to bring down, also, the bedside table and lamp. There were some further thumps and bumps and solid language involved in righting the furniture, firing up the lamp, and throwing back the bedclothes. They were, of course, too late. The invaders had retreated.

Both victims, however, had recognized the enemy.

"Well," announced Pete, in roundup tones, "I done slept in too many line shacks not to call you the brand on that herd, Billy. We've been outrode by that slicker downstairs. What will we do?"

Billy was overcome. "Seven dollars and fifty cents," he mourned, shivering to the arctic breeze whipping in from the hallway. "All that money for a stall without no winder and a humpback mattress full of bedbugs. It's purely sinful, Pete. And it ain't right, neither."

They were interrupted by an irate pounding on the wall between theirs and the adjacent room.

"For the luvva Gawd!" pleaded a weary voice, "shet up and go to sleep in there. It's four o'clock in the morning!"

Billy Hecker looked forthrightly at his comrade. "Feller's correct, Pete," he said. "It won't be more'n a hour or so to first light. You want to put out seven dollars and four bits a hour to get bed-bug bit?"

Pete Easter reached for his pants. "Heck no," he said, "let's ramble."

They dressed in swift accord. Before leaving the room Pete rapped on the intervening wall and called out loudly, "Good-by, Mister; you have drove us from our warm bed, and us but two orphaned boys what have been beat and bullied something merciless by a unnatural father and what are seeking their fortunes alone and unknown in the big city. We will all the same say a word for you in our prayers, sir."

The adjoining roomer called back for them to wait, that he had not realized their circumstances and that perhaps he could help them. But Pete was adamant.

"No," he cried, "it is too late; you have broke our spirits. Good-by, and go to Hades."

Downstairs, the clerk was no more elated to see them than he had been in the beginning. He made his ante before they had gotten off the staircase.

"You two give me one ounce of trouble," he threatened, "and I'll have the law here in thirty seconds. Jail's only around the corner, and the sheriff can hear me holler from here. And I can holler."

Pete smiled meltingly. "Shucks," he said, "no sense in doing that, mister." He eased across the lobby, still ducking his head and letting on as though in genuine pain from an overdose of the deep shys. "We only come down to take our money back," he added softly.

The clerk's mouth flew open to yell for help, but Pete had him by the collar before he could utter a sound. He hauled him out over the desk top and in behind a cluster of the potted palms. There he hung him up against the wall and started talking to him.

The old gentleman in the lobby only cocked an insomniac eye in their direction, waved his cane in clear approval of the operation, and went back to his cat-napping.

The clerk was a stubborn man and no coward. But Pete offered to lock him up in the same airtight cubicle he had rented them, and he broke down into a jelly of fear and went to begging for clemency. This he was allowed to purchase for $7.50, the exact amount Pete had given him for the Left Wing of the Presidential Suite. Putting the currency back into his brown-paper sack, Pete promised that they would always have a kind word for the Yavapai House in their travels and that, if the clerk so much as put his nose out the lobby door when they departed, they would blow his head clean off.

It was a good standard threat, one Pete had read in a paperback thriller, and it worked just fine.

Neither the clerk nor his bowlegged guests took pause to consider that the latter bore no firearms of any description. It was just a statement which sounded right to both parties under the circumstances. It was received as it was given, in good faith.

Out in the plaza once more, Billy Hecker suggested they go back down to the stage-line office and sleep out in the livery yard behind same. They each had a blanket roll behind their saddles, and it was a certain way to save $7.50. Besides, argued the Sonoita boy, they would want some local information first thing in the morning as to the best and quickest way out to Fort Whipple—this, so they could count on being first in the enlistment line, and not get left behind by being late to offer up their lives on the altar of sacred duty to their country. The stage-line agent, old Mr. Shuffman, ought to be just the one to give them this local lowdown. Also, Billy had spotted a repair wagon out in the livery yard with a nice big cozy toolbox on its bed, which would make a dandy place to bunk down, up off the ground, and so forth.

"Now, then, Pete," the slim youth concluded anxiously, "what you think of that idear?"

Big Pete looked at his small friend in frank envy. "By Gawd, Billy," he said, "you don't talk often, but when you do take off you're a finisher for sure."

"Yes, sir, thank you," said Billy. "What you think of my idear?"

"Well, sir," answered Pete honestly, "it ain't the prize winner of all time. I know this here stage line. They wouldn't give a lift to a dying man in the desert, without he had a round-trip ticket bought and paid for in advance. But I ain't got any better plan to offer, I reckon."

Billy Hecker grinned apologetically. "I know it ain't much, Pete," he said. "But it's a fact that repair rig with the big toolbox will work fair good. I figure we can shell the tools out'n it and bed down in their place toasty as tickbirds on an old bull's rump. What you say?"

Pete, never chary with his largesse, banged him between the shoulder blades. "I say you're a forty-carat genius, by gum!" he enthused. "Come on, let's make tracks for the livery yard."

At the stage depot they crept around into the rear corral, or "yard," of the line. Here they located the repair wagon in a sort of brush *ramada* tacked onto the livery barn. It was no great work to toss out the various shovels, picks, axles, spokes, spanners, and whatnot of the wagon mechanic's trade, and to so ready their couch for what was left of the night. Securing their blankets and a couple of armloads of sweet dry hay, they first made mattresses of the hay, then snugged themselves into their blankets atop it and at opposite ends of the toolbox.

But sleep, so long delayed, now grew stubborn.

Neither youth could woo the muse, and so both fell into low conversation designed to prove to the other that he, at least, could do without rest indefinitely.

The flow of this talk was valiantly afield at first. It ran to bucking horses they had known, good fellows and bad among their rodeo confreres, prices of feeders and stockers and prime slaughter steers for the coming summer, the nutrient virtues of stem-cured hay as against cut-and-baled, what zesty ladies the young Mexican females were if a man didn't mind a knife in the ribs, the best method of castrating a calf, the art of skinning rattlesnakes for belts and hatbands, how to set and throw a ground loop, heel catch, and figure eight with a show rope, and other such workaday vital statistics of their trade.

But it was all mesquite smoke.

Soon enough they fanned it away from between them and got down to rolling second cigarettes and tackling the real topic, the war in Cuba.

They agreed they weren't precisely sure what was going on between the U.S. of A. and Spain that called for a shooting fight, or why the Cubans had to be rescued by Teddy, or from what. But they were solid in their righteous rage over the Navy's recent court-of-inquiry findings about the blowing up of the battleship *Maine* in Havana Harbor, and equally worked up over the imminent prospect of being a front-line part of the 1,500-man Arizona contingent that was scheduled to be selected tomorrow and sent right on East as a separate, distinct unit of Colonel Roosevelt's cavalry. And they certainly agreed that the New York papers were entirely right, and that it was high time America opened up and showed the rest of the world that she didn't stand second at the trough to any of the other hogs, and for damned positive not to those mackerel-snapping Spaniard devils.

In this spirit of vaulting martial fervor, the two young men from Verde Valley and the Sonoita Plateau talked the stars dim, smoked up both sacks of Pete Easter's Bull Durham, and dropped off to sleep finally, just as the fighting chickens were beginning to crow over in Mexican Town, past the railroad yards.

When they awakened, it was to find the sun shining noon high in their eyes.

Alarmed, they scrambled out of the repair wagon's toolbox, only to be met by an irate stage-line agent who was not amused by the tools tossed in the manure of the livery corral nor the cut hay borrowed for bedding from his rental barn. However, Pete was equal to the menace —or essayed to be.

"Why, good morning, Mr. Shuffman, sir." He smiled. "It is charming to see you again. How has your artheritics been this spring?"

"You young fool"—Abel Shuffman scowled—"how many times I got to tell you I don't want you nor your saddlebum friends bunking in my livery barn? Now you light out'n here, Pete, and stay lit. I've a mind to send a bill to your daddy. What the heck you doing in town, boy?"

Pete told him. He added that he feared the hour was late, and that he and his friend from Sonoita would appreciate any guidance given them in the matter of getting out to Whipple barracks.

"Do you mean," said old man Shuffman, "so's you can enlist in Teddy's Terriers?"

"It's Terrors, not terriers," corrected Pete patiently. "And, yes, sir, that's what we aim to do."

"Well, boy, you'd better aim to do something else. During the night, President McKinley sent a telegraph message to Whipple, saying the number of Arizona volunteers had been cut from fifteen hundred to two hundred. I reckon you can count up what that did for the chances of your late-sleeping kind." The old man bobbed his beard feistily at the stunned youngsters. "They had them two hundred men inside the first twenty minutes. And they opened the gates at sunrise."

Billy Hecker looked at his tall, tousle-headed bunkmate and said sadly. "You will have to excuse me, Pete, but there's something I got to say."

The big cowboy nodded miserably. "Go ahead and say it," he mumbled.

"Dadblast it!" said Billy Hecker.

They got their ponies and rode slowly out of the livery yard into Gurley Street.

At the edge of town they ticked their restless mounts with their spur tips, letting them into the rocking mustang canter which eats the trail miles. Minutes later, they pulled in at the forking of the Verde Valley and Black Canyon roads.

For an awkward ten seconds neither rider found words. Then Billy Hecker nodded stiffly.

"Pete, you ever get down Sonoita or Patagonia way, you look me up. Ask anybody in Patagonia where the Hecker place is."

Pete Easter returned the nod soberly.

"Same to you, Billy," he said. "Providing you ever get over to Camp Verde or Cottonwood, our place is the Rafter J."

They exchanged a final set of nods and uneasy, shy smirks. Then they touched hatbrims and rode on, one south, one east, neither of them looking back. The dust from their ponies swirled and blew a little in the midday heat; then that, too, disappeared.

GHOST WOLF OF THUNDER MOUNTAIN

I had the story from the lips of the man it concerned most. Therefore I am confident in relating it.

This was in the Sangres country, when New Mexico was many legends younger than it is now. If I said the exact place was the ranch of Don Gaspar de Portogo on the Agua Piedra, certain *ancianos* would understand precisely what family and what rancho were intended. Yet, of course, the actual names would still be protected from today's pack of rascals and trespassers, that collective amoeba of man's curiosity which will seep in any place where the Pale One has been before them. So, call the rancho Agua Piedra and its master Don Gaspar. And call the great mountain which towers beyond the river and the grassy slopes and the juniper flats El Trueno, because that is not its true name, either, but very close to it. Ah, Old Ones, do I see you nod and smile? Certainly. You know the peak I mean.

The season was early winter. The Christmas festivities had barely commenced, upon my arrival, but at week's end had reached the carnival stage which we transplanted children of Coronado and Cabeza de Vaca regard as just the proper excitement for the Feast of the Christ Child.

Do not believe that the guest list was of far travelers and affluent, such as myself. Nothing like that. Don Gaspar was the patrón of an area larger than some states of the first American colonies. The good flock gathered at his elegant hacienda was composed principally of those he called "his children," and who in turn with vast respect addressed him as "el patrón." These would be the *vaqueros* who guarded his cattle, the *pastores* and *zagalos* who tended his sheep, the storekeepers, blacksmiths, cooks, and people of all degree who, with their broods of brown-eyed, beautiful little ones and, of course, their buxom, white-toothed women, were the "family" of Don Gaspar and of the Agua Piedra.

But this is not their story—except in a related way, like the blood of brothers is related, while different, often to strange and violent ends.

On the night of which I tell, the merrymaking had achieved that riotous pitch which the Americans mistakenly called a fandango, a wild dance without morals and leading but to mayhem and marital as well as martial strife. Well, it was true some were dancing. And many, many, were shouting on the dancers and the guitar and marimba players who lured them to their gay gyrations. If one added to this *baile* the shrieks and laughter of the children jousting to break the hanging clay baskets of bright gifts which decorated the rafters of the *sala grande*, Don Gaspar's "great room" in the hacienda, and also put into the sum of the uproar the clapping yelps of encouragement from the older ones who had passed the time of dancing in their lives, then a fact must be granted—something very like a fandango was going forward. But, then, these children of my own blood were not mingled with any but their own kind that evening. Only smiles flashed, and no knives.

Entering the *sala*, I searched at once for some less tumultuous haven. Presently, I spied it: the far side of the room where the giant fireplace gave light and warmth to the eyes and bones of the oldsters clustered there, backs hunched to the gaiety behind them, reliving their own *bailes*, far greater than this one, complaining that in that other day the children behaved themselves in a much more decorous fashion, while the young men were far more mannerly, and the young women, *Por Dios*, would not dream of showing anything like as much ankle, calf, and, God bear it witness! even *knee!*

Knowing this coterie from yesterday as the most compatible for a man of my own persuasions and, yes, admit it, of better Christmases gone by, I made my way around the crowded wall. I had reached the hearth and found my seat beside a grandly handsome octogenarian *vaquero*—or had he been, indeed, *caballero?*—and was loading my pipe when it happened.

I had never heard such a sound before, or since.

It was a long, quavering cadence of sorrow, indescribably mournful, and yet its burden came not into that room as sadness but as naked fear. Down it came through the silvered, hoar-frost air of the December night, falling from the bleak granite ramparts of El Trueno, Thunder Mountain, to spread like some chill from the other world among the gay dancers in Don Gaspar's hacienda. The pause was but that of an instant. There was a nervous shuffling of feet and coughing of throats and, here and there, a false, tittering laughter. Some young men, in bravado, spoke aloud. One child began sobbing. The older people were universally silent. It was a very disturbing moment. It passed only because Don Gaspar alertly ordered the musicians to resume at once. This they did, with an irresistible rendition of "Jalisco!"

But the spell was not broken so swiftly that I had not time to note the peculiar action of the most grizzled of the graybeards by the fire. The old fellow had started up eagerly, as the great wolf's sobbing cry had echoed down the mountain, and he had remained in a tense attitude of listening long after the final eerie note had quivered away in the distance and been lost in the returned rhythms of the marimba players.

You have guessed already that the old fellow was the one I had first been attracted to: he of the noble face and white locks to the shoulder, he beside whom I had made my seat. Presently I addressed him softly.

"The wolf calls to you, *señor;* what does he say?"

He looked sharply at me. He was certainly startled, but I also detected what might have been gratitude in the old eyes.

"You do not jest, *señor?* You do not ridicule me?"

"But of course not, Old One. I sympathize. I am in accord. I would hear what you may have to tell me."

He nodded and returned to what I thought was his endless gazing into the embers of the fire. But I had not lost him, nor he his memories.

"I was once young," he began, "even as they who click the heel and stamp the boot there where the music sounds. Rich I was in land and sheep and cattle. For wife I had one of great beauty and God-given graces. The good Christ had seen fit, as well, to bless us with a beautiful son. To this *hijo* belonged our total lives. He was the light which lit the pathways of our existence. Do you understand?"

"But of course," I bowed. "Please to continue."

"Almost daily was this son in my company, from his first birthday onward. Always was he guarded with extreme caution lest harm befall him. You see, it had befallen that, in his birth, some damage was done. My wife could bear no other child. Thus in the boy we dwelled to a degree not healthy. Eventually, such bondage as we forced upon the poor little lad became unbearable to him. He longed, just once, to wander forth without the guard of *vaqueros* which followed me, as I followed him.

" 'Please, *padre*,' he would beg of me. '*Por favor*, only this one time allow me to see the land by myself. There is something out there which seems to call to me, and I want to go and find out what it is.' "

The old man paused, shaking his silvered head.

"You will recognize this was strange talk coming from a little boy of but a few summers' age. But I was not old and wise, then, and I answered the lad impetuously and without good reason told him no.

"The springtime softened into the summer and those brief golden days of August came and went—like heat lightning, and like our youth, splendid and exciting, yet also strangely muffled and, oh! so very swift and soon gone—after that came the autumn and the red leaves and the yellow on the slopes and in the river bottoms. Soon the first fall of snow lay on the shoulders of El Trueno, mantling his palisades to the first flats and benches above the valleys.

"One day toward the fall of evening my little son was not to be found. It was full starlight when we discovered upon one of the higher flats, amid the juniper and greasewood, his small tracks, dim and lonely, leading off through the thin snowfall up the north slope of El Trueno.

As my *vaqueros* set off urgently pursuing this faint trail, slowed of course by the darkness and by the treacherous footing for their horses, the penetrating scream of the panther was heard from above us, and in the direction those tiny footprints led. And more. Even as my men and I exchanged fearful glances at this first dread sound, it was overlain by a second cry, far more compelling than that of the panther. It was *el grito del lobo*, the marrow-freezing hunger cry of the great gray timber wolf.

"Esteban Chavez, my *mayordomo*, looked at me.

" '*El lobo llama,*' he said. 'I am afraid; I think he calls to us.'

" 'Lead on, Esteban,' I replied.

"He gave me a sorrowing glance. The men did the same. But they put spurs to mounts and went on up the icy slope because they loved me and my small son.

"We came to a very dangerous switchback in the trail, then a topping-out place, studded with boulders and scrublike pines. There before our eyes lay the signs of disaster. The broad paw of the panther showed in the snow, joining the track of my son. Chavez knew this particular panther. It had had the two central toes of the left forefoot cut off by one of our traps, and Chavez and the men called this great cat La Sombra, the Shadow. The story told around the *campos* of our sheep and cattle herdsmen was that this animal was a female bigger than any male, and more—that she was not of the pure mountain lion blood, such as the panthers we knew and called pumas, but rather had for a sire some wandering Mexican jaguar male, up here in the Sangres, God knows how, on a wanderlust of hunger. This La Sombra, then, was not as other pumas, which will not harm man, not even his children or his woman. She was a killer of men and had murdered three of my own *pastores*, two of them only young boys."

Again the old man paused, his memory reaching back along the dim track of time.

"I became as one possessed," he resumed. "I threw all caution to the freezing winds and raced along the difficult trail. Suddenly, the final spark of my hope was plunged out. There, before my eyes, a third track joined the previous two. I stared down in disbelief at the great, splay-footed mark of El Lobo. We called him only that, El Lobo—*the* Wolf. And we said it that way, marking a line under the *the* with our tongue. All knew which wolf was meant: El Lobo, the most dreaded animal in New Mexico. Some said, even, that he had been feared when Oñate and Díaz and Pedro Alvarado rode here, calling all this land New Spain. Some still say this. You saw their faces but a breath ago, when the great cry sobbed down from the mountain, eh?"

"*Sí, anciano.*" I nodded. "I saw them. Pray continue."

"As you will, *señor*. I stood but a moment hypnotized by the mark of the huge foot in the snow. Then I raced on as before, caring not for La Sombra or El Lobo or for God or Christ or the Holy Ghost, even, but only for my son. I was in my own mind become greater than my Savior. Here was no place for the Prince of Peace. This was a time for the Avenger, and I was that one. My rifle was ready, my knife and my pistol, too. With my bare hands I would have attacked either beast, or both. Hope was dead but revenge was mine.

"In my madness I forged far ahead of my followers, in this manner coming first upon the tragedy.

"The way that the panther's tracks read in the snow, I knew that I stood behind the very boulder from which the bestial cat had hurled herself upon my son. I lunged beyond the fatal rock, dreading to have my worst fears confirmed, yet insane with vengeance.

"*Señor*, you will be hard-pressed to accept it. Rounding that great stone, I fell headlong over a huddled mass, measuring my length on the trail beyond. Sitting up, I beheld the monster carcass of La Sombra, rigid in that death which for her was but an experience she had meted out to countless pitiful others. Her enormous, whiskered head was thrown aside and lay at a grotesque angle. The white throat ruff was dyed crimson, the throat itself ripped open earbase to earbase."

"El Lobo?" I interjected quietly.

"The same, *señor*. In the one fearsome strike, he had smashed her down as lightning rives the mighty pine. But why, *señor?* That is what had Esteban Chavez and my men staring about into the black night and muttering as they crossed themselves.

"We searched the mountainside for any sign of my son. Nothing was discovered until, hidden in the sheltered bottom of a small *cañada*—you know, *señor*, a little cleft or rift in the mountain's flank—I found a thing which set the short hairs at the nape of my neck to bristling. There in the starlight were the marks of El Lobo's great splayed paws with the tiny footprints of my lost son, *moving side by side*. And that is the way those tracks disappeared into the darkness down the mountain's wild and desolate slope."

I let the old man pause to think his own thoughts. I did not dare to break the slender thread which was leading him back through the years.

Presently, he sighed deeply and returned to those misty times.

"Long and weary was the trailing through that night," he said. "My men were several times at the edge of exhaustion, at the rebel's point of turning back. But, as I, they loved the boy. We staggered on, our horses now behind us, led by their bridles, the way too steep and treacherous for them to bear us. Dawn found us at our trail's end. And, yes, I see that you have guessed it: the trail brought up sharply at the very door of my own great hacienda. From that place, the giant tracks of the wolf faded back into the fastness of El Trueno.

"Frantically, I rushed into my house, only to be met and silenced by my *mozos* and my women, who informed me that the boy had been snugly in his bed and sleeping these three hours!"

The old man frowned, moving his head uncertainly.

"The boy had simply come out of the blackest part of the dawn, saying he was tired and wanted to go to his bed. He seemed in no way disturbed by his harrowing experience. The following day, however, we noted an odd reluctance on his part to discuss, in any way, the adventure. That he had been with the wolf we could determine. He made several references to the 'big gray dog,' and we found upon his garments a great quantity of the black-tipped silver guard hairs of the timber wolf, as though, indeed, the great brute and my son may have lain down together to rest upon the trail at a point during their remarkable journey.

"Some time later the boy's behavior became more marked in its strangeness. We called in the priest, but he could gain no more from my son than could we, his parents and protectors. I have never since that day been the child of Mother Church that once I was. It seemed to me that here we were dealing with some very definite work of Lucifer, yet this bumbling *padre* could achieve no more than to thumb his beads and implore the Saints to send a sign by which he might know his way in the matter. Ah, what good is a God who will not better instruct his minions than that? Had I such a *mozo* or *peón* or *vaquero*, I would discharge him, or at least restrict his supply of *chiles* and *frijoles*. Well, I have wandered. Excuse me."

"It is nothing," I assured him. "All of these thoughts will pass through the mind in the remembering. I agree with you about priests. They eat too well. As you know, I am of the Faith, but I don't trust all these *padres*. I've known the sort you speak of. They ought to have been cart drivers, or charcoal burners, or again, *muleteros* or donkey women."

This pleased him fleetingly.

"Yes, they know more of boot soles than of human souls. In any event, the boy became more and more peculiar. He was to be found from time to time in the extreme cold of the patio—winter was upon us now—clad only in his night clothes gazing away toward the mountain, his face lacking all mortal animation. When I questioned him somewhat sternly about these midnight forays, he only replied softly, 'He is calling me, Father; cannot you hear him up there upon the mountain?'

" 'Who is calling?' I demanded sharply, and he answered me, still looking far away:

" '*El lobo que llora, padre*, the wolf that cries.'

"It was hopeless—and very frightening. Each night the chill wail would come sobbing down from the heights of El Trueno. Sometimes the others of us could hear it, and sometimes we could not. But the boy heard it always.

"We attempted every device. Other priests were sent in from afar, even a bishop from Coahuila. Doctors we brought in from Socorro, Santa Fe, and even Las Cruces. What use? They charged us much money and left the boy no better. I have since felt about doctors as I do about *padres*. They should all have been carpenters, like the father of Jesus."

This was the last pause, now; one sensed it.

"Well, *señor*, you have been patient. It was on an eternally damned night, brief weeks later, that my son disappeared for the final time. But this time he did not leave alone. Leading from the door of my hacienda, clearly imprinted on the new-fallen snow, side by side with those small marks of my son's tiny feet, were the great pad marks of the wolf.

"We searched the mountain again the whole night through, but you know the end, already, of this story. We did not find the boy; we did not find the wolf. Their trail faded into nothingness on the upper slopes of Thunder Mountain. The night was clear, the starlight blazing bright at this great height. Yet the tracks disappeared as if into the still black air.

"Nor did we ever find my son, *señor*. Stories there were, and continued to be: small frozen bodies found; tiny human skeletons revealed by the summer thaw high on the mountain; but always no real proof, always the body or the bones were gone when my riders and I came up to where they had been seen.

"After a certain time, my proud spirit died. My mind wandered, and my riches with it. Even my name was forgotten. It still is forgotten. These happy ones in this room do not remember me, only my story.

"It is as well. Do you know what night it was upon which the boy last left me, the night we found the wolf tracks leading him away from that door beyond the dancers, there? It was on the same night as this present one, *señor;* the same night and in this very hacienda, then mine, that it happened. Do you wonder, now, that I start up when El Lobo calls upon the mountain? Do you wonder that I hold my hand to my ear, listening to hear if it is my name he calls at last? Well, *señor*, the time of waiting is done. Tonight I heard my name. I am content, my friend. Already it grows overlong since I have seen my little son. It will be a glad meeting on the far mountain. Remember that. Let there be no sadness, now, when the wolf has called again."

I started to say something to him, as his words trailed off, but my own words never left my lips.

A log dislodged in the fireplace, sending up a shower of sparks. The noise of the revelers grew unaccountably quiet. I shook myself to ward off a sensation of creeping cold, or of a frosty draft of air. I even looked to see if some overheated dancers had opened the great oaken door of the hacienda. They had not.

Yet suddenly the merrymakers froze in their positions. A popping ember echoed in the stillness. From high above an eerily beautiful wolf howl sounded on Thunder Mountain. At the first notes of the call, the old man by my side glanced upward in the direction of El Trueno. But as the final strains sobbed from the heights, he was no longer looking toward the mountain. He was leaning back with a gentle smile of peace, and I realized the gallant soul had fled. There remained, however, one element of that departure which puzzled me. It was a thing I had to make sure of in my own mind, for the sake of my own peace.

I went quickly to the oaken door of the hacienda. When no one was watching, I opened it and stepped outside. A new snow was falling. It lay all about the ranch yard innocent of disturbance except for a singular distinct impression upon its starlit surface. From the hacienda's doorstep, stretching away into the winter darkness toward the waiting midnight snows of El Trueno, lay three sets of footprints: one set were those of a very old man, one those of a very young lad, and one those of a larger American timber wolf than I had ever seen.

Even as I stared at the ghostly footprints of the three companions, their trackmarks were beginning to fade beneath the increasing fall of the snow. When I returned to the big room of the hacienda and was told the old man had indeed passed on, I went again to the oaken door and looked out into the night.

The tracks were gone.

The snow beyond the ancient doorstep lay clean of any mark, and I never repeated this story, then or since.

Many winters afterward, as I studied a letter of congratulations addressed to me by my colleagues of the government biological survey, I had cause to think once more of my peculiar experience at Don Gaspar's hacienda. The government letter concerned my lifelong work in the habits of the Western timber wolf. It expressed particular praise for my papers describing all the known calls and cries of the animal, and of course it was this latter fact which returned my memory to the Agua Piedra ranch and the snow-shrouded ramparts of El Trueno.

Ah, wait. Do not smile understandingly and turn away, young friends. Consider first this matter.

In spite of the position of authority granted me by my colleagues in the study of the American wolf, I have never succeeded in identifying the species which uttered the incredibly sad and eerie lament which swept the winter air over Don Gaspar's hacienda that Christmas night so long ago.

Honors and letters from wise men do not make a man wise.

The great animal whose tracks I saw leading toward El Trueno, and whose howl I heard wafting down from that snowy peak, remains for me, as for the most ignorant peon on the slopes of the Agua Piedra, The Ghost Wolf of Thunder Mountain.

A BULLET FOR BILLY THE KID

When the child was coming, the mother glanced beyond the filthy-handed midwife tending her and saw the shadowed form of Asaph standing in the door.

"Who is there?" she asked, and the midwife, turning, saw no one.

"Shut up," she said, "and work."

But the man nodded and said softly, "I am Asaph. I heard your cries. I want to help you with the child."

The mother nodded, sighed, and lay back. "Thank you," she said. "You're a stranger. I don't know you."

"I am a stranger," answered Asaph, "but you know me."

The woman upon the rumpled bed began to cry. The baby was breech to, and the hurt of it within her was very great. Asaph came to her side.

"Don't be afraid," he said. "Your son will come alive."

He laid cool and slim fingers on her brow, and the woman grew quiet.

"You said my son," she murmured. "How do you know it will be a boy?"

"Shut up, curse you!" growled the midwife. "Stop that crazy talking and twisting. I just had him by the ankles and he got away from me. Now lay still or I'll belt you one."

"You say it's a boy, too," groaned the woman. "How do you know that?"

"I can tell by the bottoms of the feet. Now shut your mouth and bear down. I got my floors to scrub yet."

The mother looked up at Asaph, and the stranger

nodded to her as if to say yes, now is the moment. She closed her eyes, and in a burst of agony the baby came. It was a boy, short and wide of body, big of head, and very homely.

"Call him Billy." Asaph smiled, and when the mother nodded in agreement and opened her eyes to thank the stranger, he was gone.

"What are you going to name him?" asked the midwife, holding the ugly infant by the heels to slap the breath of life into the rasping lungs.

"Didn't you hear?" said the woman, frowning. "Billy."

"Better make it Beelzebub." The slattern scowled. "He sure took the Devil's own time getting here."

When the boy was three the father, a drink raddled rogue, moved his family from New York westward. His urge was to improve his fortune, but he died along the way or disappeared, and the mother continued drifting westward with the boy, making her own way. It was a far journey. Its directions came to her from time to time, and she followed them. Something told her where and when to bend her path, that was all. She thought often, along the way, of the soft-voiced Asaph who had helped her to bear young Billy. Many times she wished the gentle stranger would reappear so that she might ask his advice on what course next to take; the boy was growing now and needed a father.

Swiftly and with hardness the years wore on. The boy was eight or perhaps nine. Long since, his mother had taken another man. But the boy would have been better off with no father at all than Antrim, the dull-eyed lout the woman chose or who, more likely, chose the woman.

From settlement to settlement the three wandered, and from sorrow to sorrow. The woman lost hope, the boy, happiness.

It was on a gusting autumn night, when the mother sat waiting long after midnight for her drunken second mate, that a knock came at the door of the shabby hotel wherein she and the brute and the boy existed.

She did not think before she called out, "Who is

there?" Yet the instant the words fell she knew who it was and at once cried, "Oh, I'm so glad; come in, come in!"

And it was he of course: Asaph the stranger.

Now, however, in some way he did not seem so mysterious. She accepted him into the shabby room, warning him only not to awaken the boy who slept on a straw pallet in the corner.

"You know"—the stranger smiled—"you never told me your name."

"It's Kathleen, Kathleen Antrim now."

"And the boy? He is still Billy, as we agreed?"

"Yes. Some call him Billy Antrim; he calls himself Billy Bonney."

"Ah," said Asaph softly, "exactly."

There was a moment's silence. Asaph studied Kathleen Antrim.

"Take the boy," he said, "and go with him down into New Mexico. Here is money. It is sufficient to establish you. A boardinghouse would be good, I think. Yes, begin with that." He paused once more. "You will not like Santa Fe," he said, "and will end in Silver City."

"And you?" she said.

"I will meet you there. I have no choice."

"No choice?" She was puzzled, a little uneasy.

"It's the boy." He smiled. "Would you want me to forsake him?"

"No," said Kathleen Antrim. "You've been kind to us."

"How has the boy been?" asked Asaph softly. "He seems well, strong. There's something to him, too. He's not ordinary."

Kathleen Antrim looked down at the sleeping Billy.

The youth's piggish nose tilted upward absurdly. Freckles spattered his impish face. Weak-chinned, the upper teeth protruding, rabbitlike, the eyes wide-set and angled for good humor, he radiated even in slumber the spirit of tough Irish carefreeness, the charm of the leprechaun and larrikin combined.

"You're right." She sighed. "And, ah, how lucky he is to have a man like yourself who knows his inner spark!"

The boy stirred in his sleep, rooting in the sour blanket which twined his short form.

"Shhh," cautioned Asaph. "Have you told the lad of me?"

"No."

"As well. Leave that to me. I will know the time for it."

The woman nodded. "When that time comes," she said, "will you also tell me of yourself?"

He caught her eyes, locking them. "Nothing has changed," he answered her. "You know who I am, and why I am here."

"No, no, I don't," she protested. "Honest to God!"

"Don't say that again." Asaph rasped the words, white-lipped; then at once was gentle and kind as ever. "We've no need for oaths between us, Kathleen Antrim," he explained. "We're old friends."

"Then you still want me to take Billy and go to New Mexico?"

"I have given you the money to do so, have I not?"

She started to protest that he had *not* given her the money. But before she could, she realized Asaph was no longer in the room. Something else, however, was in that room which had not been there before the stranger's soft knocking at the door.

In Kathleen Antrim's outstretched hands lay fifty $20 gold pieces.

In Silver City, life was a little better for them. Kathleen, living still with Antrim, worked as Asaph had instructed her, taking in boarders, and did well enough. But the boy, bright as new-vein copper, had some handicap of restless blood against the humdrum challenge of the schoolroom. Ignorant, raffish, rootless, he drifted the streets of Silver City like some runty brown-haired coyote whelp. And like the little brush wolf that he was, he learned the lessons of life from a sharper teacher than the weary headmaster of the camp's wet-pine and canvas schoolhouse.

Not yet nine years old, he understood that men drank themselves sick and stupid; that women sold themselves;

that money was power, greed universal, gambling profitable to the dishonest; and that of all the virtues necessary to survival in that harsh time and place the greatest two were cunning and raw courage.

In the bars, the bistros, the parlors of the mining camp the boy studied with a hero's application. He ran errands, carried messages, made assignations, racked pool balls, cleaned spittoons—whatever needed doing that would earn him the company of older men and women. He became welcome where the ordinary child would have been dusted out the swinging doors with the swamper's broom. And in all of this he managed, by the magic of his buck-toothed grin, his eagerness to toil, his rash courage and undoubted Irish gifts of blather and of blarney, to win the championing not only of the seamy set but of the very proper citizenry as well.

Where he passed upon the streets, old ladies smiled at him. They did not remember his name but had felt his sturdy hand in help with some heavy burden, or in crossing a crowded street, and they remembered *him*. All women, in fact, were his particular devotion. And of all women his mother was the major passion of his chivalry.

Some records say the Antrims lived in Silver City a sum of four years. If this is so, it does not agree with the ledger kept by Asaph, who had it reckoned but three seasons.

Yet, by either reckoning, the boy was twelve or thirteen and the year 1872 when the stranger kept his word and came again, and in the night, to the appointment he had made in Silver City.

It was a raw night. Gusts of wind whipped a fine rain through the mud gutters. Down Main Street, late in getting home, came Kathleen Antrim. With her was the boy, Billy. In the shadows of the alleyway separating the saloon from the livery stable, stood Asaph. It took two looks to see him, then a third to be certain he was there.

Asaph, seeing Billy and his mother, turned his attention from them to the saloon. As his glance fell upon the slatted doors, they burst apart and a drunk stumbled forth to stand swaying on the board walk. He had to give way for Kathleen Antrim, but as she passed he made an insulting remark which Billy heard.

The lad was at him like a ferret to a bear, so wrong was the pairing of sizes. But, armed with a cobble from the roadway, the boy might have brained the weaving sot had it not been for Asaph. The latter moved from the alleyway in time to lay his hand on Billy's back-drawn arm.

"Wait," he said, in his soft voice which so compelled the listener to obey. "I will help you."

The drunk by now had recovered from his fog enough to stagger over to Billy.

And in the same moment Kathleen Antrim had recognized Asaph. She opened her mouth to say his name, glad in her heart to see him, when he lay the slender long finger to his lips in the remembered gesture, warning her to be quiet.

"You sniveling guttersnipe," mumbled the drunk to Billy. "Pick up a rock on me, will you?" He steadied himself to seize the boy. Asaph glanced again at the saloon doors. And again they opened to bring a second customer, but not an unsteady one, out upon the board walk.

Ed Moulton, a good man, took the sodden drunk by the collar and flung him into the muck of the gutter. He then tipped his hat to Kathleen Antrim and went his separate way. If he saw Asaph, he did not remark the fact.

More peculiarly, even, young Billy paid no heed to the soft-spoken stranger. He simply took Kathleen Antrim by the arm and said, "Come along, Ma, we'd best get shut of here." And when she held back to question Asaph—she had heard him speak to Billy—Asaph only put his finger to his lips and smiled.

"It's not time yet," was all he said.

"Ma, come on. Don't stand here worrying and muttering about that drunk. That mud and water will sober him up just fine." Billy gave her arm another tug, and she went along with him, shaking her head. At the corner she looked back. The board walk in front of the saloon was deserted. Only the lamp shine and the slick of the rain occupied it. Asaph was gone.

"Bottoms up," said Ed Moulton, raising his shot of red-eye whisky. His companion nodded and downed his drink. The noise and crowd in Joe Dyer's place was about the same as it had been the night three weeks earlier when the drunk had insulted Billy Bonney's mother. There was this difference, however: the drunk had two friends with him this time and was sober. He came into the saloon, and Moulton did not recognize him or his companions. They were able to get behind the friendly Silver Citian. Had not Ed's drinking pal seen them circling, Moulton would have been unwarned of their attack. As it was, these were bad *hombres*, all three, and Ed no fighter. He had time to wheel about and get his hands up, then he was on the floor getting his ribs kicked in.

The crowd closed in as such crowds will, not caring who was being hurt so long as someone was spilling blood—not theirs, of course, and the winner would undoubtedly stand a round on the house.

No one saw the small boy who burrowed through the circle of cheering oafs. But the boy, reaching the inside of the circle, was in time to see the brute who had passed the foul remark to his mother sweep up a chair and poise it to crush the skull of Ed Moulton from behind.

Someone saw Billy then because of the flash of the bared knife's blade in his hand, as he leaped in toward the hulking sneak who threatened Moulton from the rear. Several saw the bright arc of the blade as the boy swept it upward into the vitals of the bully, once, twice, three times, ripping on each thrust. And all there heard the grunt of shock come out of the man, saw the color drain out of his face, saw his mouth move with no sound coming from it, then saw him sag and turn to tallow in the knees, sliding down upon the sawdust of the floor.

"It's the Bonney kid!" someone shouted. "Stop him! Where'd he go?"

"Out the front," answered Asaph, sitting at a table in a darkened corner by the bar. "He went by me only this instant."

The crowd surged out upon the board walk, the barkeep, even, following the exodus. On the floor writhed the bully, dying, and his two comrades, peering down, saw this in the rotten color of his face, and they went out the back way of the saloon very quickly.

Asaph lifted the soiled cloth of the table where he sat. "All right," he said to the fearful boy crouched beneath the table, "out the back way after those two. Quick, before the crowd spills back in from out in front."

He led the way for Billy, ducking down below the bar, following it to the alleyway exit behind Joe Dyer's place, and the boy went after him closer than a shadow's shadow. Outside, Asaph pulled the lad into a dank hiding space between beer barrels, empty whisky cases, and piled street refuse.

"Listen," he instructed him, "my name is Asaph. I knew your mother in New York. You could ask her, but there is no time. You can't go home again, boy; from here you follow me. Or, if you please, I follow you. It's in the viewpoint."

"I don't get you, mister," panted the lad. "You want to help me, or what? Why'd you get me out of there?"

"That man is dying, Billy boy. He will be dead before the people are all returned from the board walk. You killed a man in cold blood. The owlhoot places wait for you, and nowhere else will you be safe. Do you understand that much?"

"Yes, sir." Billy gulped.

"Now, boy," Asaph said, "there is no time for anything but flight. There is a place where we will rendezvous —Camp Bowie—do you mark it in your memory?"

"Yes, I've heard the name and I can find it. How come you to help me anyhow?"

"We're traveling the same road." Asaph smiled. He touched the boy on the shoulder, pointing down the alleyway to the south, where the town's few lights winked quickly out and only the black sagebrush waited. "Go that way," he said. "Here come the people from the bar. I will give them another bad direction. Run, Billy, run!"

Billy was gone, then, and in a moment Asaph was telling the first of the drinkers from Joe Dyer's that he had seen the boy run north, going toward Main Street and his mother's boardinghouse, no doubt.

When some of the men, disgusted, returned from their

brief search to demand some further information of the stranger who had twice sent the hunt astray, the latter was nowhere to found.

Only the wind whistled up and down the empty alley—and even seemed to laugh a little on the way.

For three days Billy wandered without shelter or food. On the fourth day, toward evening, he came across a Mexican lad of his own age. The dark-skinned youth took him home, hiding him in the loft of the family goat pen. It was out of the wind there, and, smell though it might, it was warm in the soft prairie hay, and the friendly bleating of the animals kept their visitor calmed. The Mexican boy brought him tortillas and cold bean mash from the rancho kitchen, even some steaming coffee in a tin can. When Billy went on from that place he took with him the loyalty for the dusky children of the *monte* which was to become a dedication with him; "my people" he would call them, and they would name him fondly "our Billito."

Drifting on, skirting all settlements, he worked his way toward Camp Bowie. He found a new friend, another frontier waif such as himself, also wandering the wasteland. The other boy would not tell Billy his name, and so Billy, never one to be daunted by such details, said, laughing, "All right, we'll just call you Nameless Joe, and leave it lay at that."

The two boys, astride a sore-backed mare stolen from a white squatter's stock pen—Billy would not steal from Mexicans—came at last to Camp Bowie. There they waited for Asaph, but he did not come. Some soldiers, though, befriended them. Much impressed by the bravery of the lads to be striking out alone in such a hard country, the troopers furnished them a rusted rifle and pistol, with some verdigrised ammunition, and warned them to "keep an eye out for the sneaking 'Paches," as the Indians had been bad recently.

They were in Arizona, now, their path leading onward deeper into that neighboring territory.

On a bright sunny morning two days out of Camp Bowie, they came upon three Indians. Though Apaches, they were "friendlies," and Billy knew enough of "Injun talk" to understand plainly their identity. He laughed with them, trading smile for smile, warm word for warm word. When the Indians thought they had gained the confidence of the boys, they gave them a generous gift of pipe tobacco and rode on happily, singing the Apache morning prayers of thanks for a fine day. The bells on their twelve pack animals loaded with fur pelts for the post trader at Camp Bowie tinkled and made a most pleasant music in the clear and tangy sunshine.

"Nameless Joe," said Billy, "do you suppose this old cannon will shoot where it is held?" and with the question he pulled the rusted gun and leveled it and fired it point-blank into the back of the chanting Indians. The gun hit where it was held. The braves, all struck in spine or skull, toppled from their mounts and lay quiet.

"By jings!" crowed Billy. "We have struck it rich; we are in the fur business, Nameless Joe."

Nameless Joe nodded and said nothing. But he was thinking very hard. A white man knifed into the sawdust of Joe Dyer's saloon? Three friendly red men dead of gunshots in the back, fired with a laugh and no regrets? This was a good friend? A business partner?

Billy had used four bullets only on the Apaches. He had two shots remaining in the rusted gun. Nameless Joe kept thinking of those two moldy green bullets all day long. That night, when only the stars watched, he fled the camp on foot.

Next daybreak Billy, finding him gone, merely laughed and called him "Faithless Joe," and forgot him. But turning to fetch his horse, he heard behind him the rattle of a pebble. Whirling he fired at the mounted man who had come up so silently. As he did, and through the smoke, he recognized the rider and stammered out hoarse apology for the mistake.

"No harm done." Asaph smiled, getting down from the gaunt and pale horse he rode. "I'm pleased to see you so alert."

"I'm glad I missed you," Billy said, but was uneasy in the claim. He had not missed that easy point-blank belly shot. He knew he had not missed it. But he could see no hole in Asaph's coat or vest where such a shot would have centered. Nor did the soft-voiced stranger offer explanation of the odd condition. "I mean," said Billy, "seeing you're a friend of my mother's and—well, you know."

"Yes," agreed Asaph, "I know."

He regarded the homely, half-defiant urchin of the owlhoot trail with some bemusement.

"If you travel on in this Indian country with those horses and the peltries that they bear," he said, "other Indians will see you, and I need not describe the rest for a boy as smart as you."

"What do you suggest?" said his small listener, blue eyes watching him sharply.

"I'll buy them from you," said Asaph. "I know a place near here where they may be disposed of quietly."

"Hah! There's five–six hundred dollars' worth there!"

"Easily," said Asaph. "Nor do I propose to cheat you." He took a doeskin money pouch from his coat, hefting it. Tossing it to Billy, he said, "Here's a thousand dollars. You've made a good start. Buy yourself an outfit of the first order. Everything you need. But travel on; don't turn back to Bowie."

Billy looked into the pouch, saw the dull winking of the minted gold, knew better than to count the ancient coins.

"Until the next time," Asaph smiled, turning his pale horse.

"Wait!" Billy called. "I will fetch my nag, and we can ride together for a ways. There's things I want to ask of you—and maybe say some others for myself."

He ran around the clump of mesquite scrub where his mustang stood picketed, with saddle on, the way all horses stand where riders slumber along the owlhoot. But when he kicked the little beast into a gallop to spur back and join Asaph, he saw a thing which brought him to stop the pony and sit staring off, badly startled.

Asaph was riding away, leading the string of Apache pack animals which he had purchased from Billy. This was as it should be, for he had not answered Billy that he would wait for him. But the boy still sat and stared and shook his head, and muttered under his breath. That was Asaph, sure enough. And that was Billy's Apache Indian pack string following him. But Billy had not been thirty seconds pulling picket pin and scrambling to saddle on his own mount. Yet Asaph and the Apache ponies were already disappearing past the crest of Mescalero Ridge, a rocky outcrop on the trail *fifteen miles to the east.*

Billy lived eight years from those first kills and never spared the gun; and in all that time, beginning with the friendly Indians, he never shot from the front or straightaway, the legend notwithstanding.

If he called out a man, he called him so with his trigger finger already closing, his small hand already gripped about the walnut handle of the Colt self-cocker .41 which had become his favored weapon in those latter desperate days.

When faced as several times he was by men of equal skill, Billy always quit. He would grin and give way and make as if the whole thing had been a joke from the first hard word. Later he would curse, alone, where none could hear his ugly oath to dry-gulch yet another poor devil who had offended his private code, which was whatever he wanted it to be, so bent to fit each crime.

He never killed a man he did not swear deserved the death

Yet Asaph, following him patiently, watching the way his life ran, as he had promised Billy's mother he would do, saw no killing any court would call justified or label, in the legal term, as self-defense.

Asaph grew jaded with the chore. Kathleen Antrim, dead since 1874, could never know the full bad color of her runted son, and if the gentle stranger quit the trail now, when she was gone, what harm in that? Would that warped life begun in the New York tenement run any different skein should Asaph drop its ugly stitch where presently it spun across the Arizona sands?

Ah, but that was not the question.

This was no boy of Kathleen Antrim's here; this was child, Billito. He would not abandon him.

The numbers of the notches grew from four to five, the fifth a soldier blacksmith at Fort Bowie, the same place called "camp" when Nameless Joe and Billy Bonney rode that way in '72.

When the blacksmith lay staring at the sky, eyeballs blank and glazing, there were again no witnesses—or there were none who cared to come forward.

"The rascal cheated me," claimed Billy, "and was to boot a sullen bully. If, as they say, I shot him short, then let the liar front me with it to my face."

But he was talking to the wind, or to the dust which stirred beneath it, or to the cold and blinking stars. For men no longer smiled back at him, though women still defended valiantly each ambush by the buck-toothed boy who, in his turn and just as senselessly, championed their sex against all charges. That was one of his two remaining loyalties in life, to protect the female kind. But men, looking down on evidence of murder mirrored in the open eyes of other men shot from behind, were not amused by amorosity or proof of mother love.

Billy found Arizona's climate warming unseasonably after the Fort Bowie affair. No more did he feel comfortable in the land of the Chiricahuas and the U.S. Cavalry. Surely, things would be better for "Billito" back in New Mexico, where he would be with "his people," with dark-skinned Carlos, Juan, Roberto, and their steadfast clan. So determined, he rode at once and swiftly for the territorial line. But quickly as his pony ran, another paler horse was there before him.

Billy was heading for Animas, across the line, and over Antelope Pass. With the Peloncillos range behind him he would feel at home, and he could see the saw-toothed spine of that familiar rampart only miles ahead as his mount brought him down to the Cochise Crossing of San Simon Creek, on the Arizona side.

It was here that he found Asaph watering his bony white.

"By God," cried Billy, "this is luck!"

"Be still!" ordered Asaph sternly. "I don't like oaths."

"Oaths?" The youth laughed. "You don't like oaths? That's a hot one! You don't mind fencing Apache peltries robbed off dead Injuns, but you wince at cuss words, eh?"

"I didn't say cuss words; just don't use that oath again"

"All right, heck, who cares." The blue-eyed fugitive grinned. "Here I am running from the Cavalry and meet up with an old friend of my mother's just in time to swap him my blowed horse for his fresh one, and we're talking oaths!"

With the grin, he produced the famed .41 Colt.

"Now, old friend of my mother's," he said, waving the weapon, "get off that bone pile horse of yours and hand him over to me, easy like. From here, me and you leave different tracks. You take my nag, and when the soldier boys catch up to you just tell them I stole your plug and left you mine. Now, hop it!"

Asaph made no move to get down. "I doubt," he said, "that you would want to ride this steed. He goes a gait not many men sit happily."

"Get off'n him!" snarled Billy, the time for smiles long past. "I missed you once, blast you; it won't happen again."

"No it won't," agreed Asaph softly.

He swung down from the gaunt-ribbed white and handed up the reins to Billy, still mounted on his own rangy bay.

Billy moved to take the reins and, in the motion, his hand touched that of Asaph. He recoiled from the contact, his impish face a fleeting picture of startlement.

Asaph stood looking up at him. "What is it?" he said.

"Your hand," answered Billy, scowling now, recovering. "You got a hand like ice!" He broke off, defensive anger replacing the moment's panic started up within him by the touch of Asaph's hand. "Go to the devil." He grimaced, waving aside the proffered reins.

"A reasonable suggestion," said Asaph, amused, "but I've little mood to humor it. Come along, boy, this time we'll ride a way together. The soldiers are too close for us to risk different paths."

Billy knew the troopers to be hard behind him. Yet, of a sudden, he did not want Asaph with him. "Listen," he urged, "I don't mean to draw you into this pot. You didn't call for no cards in the hand. No use declaring yourself in at this late date, *amigo*. I killed a man back yonder."

"I know," said Asaph. "I was there and saw you do it."

"You was? The heck! I never seen you."

"You shot him in the back of the head and turned his pockets out." The other shrugged. "He cheated you, all right; he had no money on his person."

"Son of a gun!" said Billy Bonney uneasily. "Let's go."

Asaph remounted, and together his white horse and young Bonney's bay splashed over the rippling shallows of Cochise Crossing. But there was something odd about that fording.

Two horses went into the stream and two came out of it on the far side, yet only one line of hoof prints appeared in the damp sand of the exit, to lead away from water's edge toward New Mexico—those of Billy Bonney's bay.

"Now," said Asaph, "I must leave you."

They sat their horses, not upon the trail to Animas but south-turning, through the Alamo Hueco Mountains and into Chihuahua, old Mexico. Billy nodded. He was still tense, still apprehensive. Yet Asaph had convinced him.

"Well," the young killer admitted, "I can't rightly dispute it with you. If you say I'd ought to go down there to Chihuahua City, then I'll go. I ain't forgot you told me to stay away from Fort Bowie, and look what happened."

It was Asaph's turn to nod. He thought how simple most men were. Did it not occur to this blue-eyed boy of his that Asaph understood he would do what he was told *not* to do, and that therefore the reason for so telling him was served precisely?

No, never.

This was what made it so easy for Asaph in the world. He had never had to sweat and toil to make his way, but only to direct and misdirect others to the end that they perspired and labored in his cause. In a way, this Billy Bonney lad sought the same conveniences. He would not take steady work, or work of any decent kind. Of the many unmentionable things he would do and had done, honest work was never one. Shady travail he would seize eagerly upon. He would run his lungs out on an evil errand, or peel his fingers to the tarsals, should the chore promise ill-gotten gain. But to hew to the line, sun to dark, for pay? Hah, not Billy Bonney!

Well, the pity was that the lad, with all the appetite for wrong, had not the head to handle his stomach. The lack of brains was ever Billy's problem.

"All right," Asaph said, breaking the pause, "it is good that you have learned so early. It will make the rest an easier thing for both of us."

"What the heck are you talking about?" Billy scowled. "What rest of what?"

Asaph calmed him with a smile.

"The rest of 'us,' " he said, good-humoredly. "It seems we continue to meet along the trail, lad. Why not imagine we shall meet again, and continue thus to meet throughout your days?"

"*My* days?" Too long in the brush and on the lam to miss slight trail signs, Billy frowned again. "What about your days? Or ours? Why just mine?"

"Why not just yours? Do you know anyone else's more important to the plan?"

"Cuss it all, what plan? You talk like a man with mush in his mouth. I ain't got no plan with you."

Asaph laughed aloud. It was a strange sound, not unmusical, however, and indeed attractive in a nameless way. "I mean to say, what life is more important to you than your own? Is it mine?"

"Well, not hardly."

"Exactly the point, wild boy; and who has been more tender of your days than I?"

Billy chewed his Irish upper lip and scowled. "Well, if you say so. I reckon now with Ma gone, and barring my Mex friends in the chaparral, you're all that cares for me or gives a hoot."

"Precisely."

"I'll do it then, Asaph. Chihuahua City it is, and I will stay there till you send for me."

Asaph nodded quickly. "A messenger will come in my name," he said. "Wait for him."

They parted, the deal agreed. But Billy Bonney was of wily mind, if limited. No sooner was he out of sight of

Asaph than he wheeled his horse once more to the west. Instead of going by the left-hand trail to Chihuahua, he went the right-hand road toward Sonora.

Martínez was the dealer's name. What town it was in old Sonora is not remembered. But Billy was there and the game went against him, or so the Mexican witnesses said.

For Billy's part, he later insisted, faithful to his pattern in such affairs, "He peeled them from the inside of the pack. A Spanish deck is still a Spanish deck, to be dealt from fair and square; I was being robbed right there in front of everybody. More than that, the crazy fool laughed at me. Nobody laughs at Billy Bonney, not and steals the pot from him, by jing! Sure I shot him. And it's a black lie if they tell you I didn't give him no more chance than he did me. I called him and he laughed, and I let him have five rounds under the table. He could have played it fair and been alive today."

Whatever Billy's story, he was in deep trouble, far from the border and having killed his first Mexican. Now the last of his two loyalties was no more, and when the word came up out of old Sonora that Billito had killed Martínez *beneath the table*, then the old security he had always known among his brown-skinned "people" was a thing of the receding past. From that day the Mexican folk were not so sure of their beloved Billito, even if their women still believed in him, and Billy could no longer count on disappearing into the *monte*, when the humor suited him or the sheriff was too close behind.

Indeed he might never have left Sonora alive, but for the timely interference of one Malquierdes Segura, a Mexican youth of his own age and his equal, as well, in wild daring.

Segura it was, who, seeing Billy flee the dim cantina with his Colt .41 still smoking, beckoned him into the darkened doorway of his sweetheart's home, admitted him into that house, and hid him there until the hue and cry had died away.

When the excited townsmen rushed on by and vanished down the dusty street shouting after him in Spanish to wait and be hung or, better, be shot while escaping, like a decent fellow would do in the same guilty straits, Segura turned to Billy with a grin as lunatic and scary as his own.

"*¡Ay, Chihuahua!*" He laughed. "That was a near thing!"

"Yes indeed," responded Billy, bowing with mock gravity. "*Muchísimas gracias.* Permit me to present myself: I am Billy Bonney."

He of course spoke flawless Spanish, and when he had told Segura who he was, the Mexican youth's dark face lit up.

"Why," he said, "that is a wondrous thing; I have been looking for you. I was told I'd find you here."

"You? Looking for me? How is that, *amigo?*"

Quick to take suspicion always, Billy was immediately on guard.

"Asaph sent me," was all Segura said; yet in those three words, or with them, he might as well have struck a knife in his listener.

"Asaph!" breathed Billy. "That circling buzzard, why does he trail me so? He—wait—you lie, he told me to go to Chihuahua!"

"That is so. He said as much to me, also. However, that is not my affair, *compañero.* Asaph sent me to get you out of here, and that I will do. *¡Basta!* Come on. That crowd of barking dogs will be yelping back this way before you know it."

"But, blast it," protested Billy, "I'm not sure of you."

"Bah, why worry about me? Would you want to bring shame on the house of my sweetheart, a poor defenseless girl?"

"No, God forbid. I would never harm a woman. Let's go."

Go they did, and quickly, following narrow paths and secret trails through the hills that only wild cattle trod, traveling toward Chihuahua and the city to which Asaph had originally instructed Billy to proceed. Billy was much taken with Segura, and he with Billy. But the Mexican would not talk about Asaph, vowing that he knew too little of the latter to warrant a conversation, and saying, too, that it mattered not the least in any way. The important thing was that he and Billy Bonney had found one another and would make an outlaw pair to bring fond memories to the dark eyes of all the *chiquitas* twixt Auga Prieta and Guadalupe!

"By jing!" vowed Billy, touching up the trim gray mare, La Chispa, which Segura had provided for him. "Me and you will bust the bank for sure, providing you can pick a lock or a hideout house or a pretty girl as good as you can a horse!"

"That mare," shouted back Segura, "cost Asaph five hundred in Spanish gold—I saw him pay it—for it was I who told him where she was for sale."

Billy laughed with pure good hellish feeling. The lights of the town lay far behind, and with them all noise of any play for vengeance over the monte dealer Martínez. What luck to find a side-kick like Segura, and a mount the order of this hotblood iron gray which moved beneath him fluid and wildly swift as mountain water in cascade or quicksilver beading bright in racing pearls. Santa Maria! this was more like it was in the good old days. It was certain he owed Asaph more than any man could pay. But he would find a way to do it. For Billy Bonney settled his debts, whether with lead or gold, and he would see that he did not stand short with that cussed stranger when the last pack had been cut, and dealt, and all cards turned face up for cashing-out.

"I guess," he said aloud, and after some delay, in answer to Segura, "I owe that Asaph dude aplenty. This here mare's a holy terror: she don't run, she *transfers* through the air."

"Something like that," said Segura, and laughed softly as he said it. "You know, Billito, that mare she is the half-sister to that pale bone pile Asaph rides."

"A lie!" cried Billy. "Dang you, that's a lie!"

Segura turned his dark face from the moon. Billy could not see it, shadowed so. But he could hear the words which came, lisping with the Spanish laugh.

"A lie you say? No kin to Asaph's steed? Ah, *amigo*, so much to learn, so little time in which to learn it, eh?

Do this: the next time that you see that horse of Asaph's, mark the trackline that he leaves. *Then* tell Segura that he lies."

Martínez was the sixth man Billy killed.

It seemed his death gave other ideas to the latter. Chihuahua City also had a monte game, but this time the dealer was not charged. It was the keeper of the bank who was waylaid going home in the black hours of the dawn. If he were killed no one could ever prove, nor could theft of the money he was carrying be noted to Billy's account. The man *and* the money simply disappeared from the middle of the town and were not seen again. But there was a witness:

"The rascal cheated Billito and—well, who better to repay the loss than the banker of the game? If he disappeared what difference, so long as the debt was discharged? Did anyone hear Billito complain past that night of being shorn in Chihuahua? Never! He was always fair about such things."

So said Malquierdes Segura, who told a good story then and later, too.

The Chihuahua banker was number seven and, like number six, a Mexican. How Segura balanced this account is business which he never jotted down. Seemingly he was a child of universal blood, the same as Billy Bonney. Besides, he had done no crimes, only transported Billy in these matters, guided him, or furnished horseflesh none could catch, such trivial things, no more.

Billy, past that year of 1876, was likened by some who knew him from Silver City, and the firming influence of Kathleen Antrim, to a trusty stock dog which has taken to killing sheep.

The taste of the victim seemed to swell his appetite, not diminish it. And, like a dog gone wild, he commenced to kill senselessly, to strike at anything which moved or made a shadow or uttered a faint bleat along the trail he rode. In this manner the dead ones, eight through twelve and past twelve to pushing twenty, piled up behind him.

There were lies told of the list, of course. More men

were added to it than deserved the fate. Circumstances surely were not always such as to place full blame on Billy. Indeed, as always with such warriors of the owlhoot tribe, far from it. He became a hero in his own time according to the legend. He killed to protect the poor. He killed in defense of frightened womanhood. He killed the wicked in the name of the good. He was generous. He gave away his bloody wealth. He traveled with no gold saved for himself. Had he a bone he would share it with a hungry dog. Had he no bone for the poor brute, he would go to the kitchen of the nearest rich man and fetch him one. No little man need fear with Billy near, nor need his sister cringe in terror, nor his old mother know want.

These were Billito's people, these *pobrecitos* of the *monte.*

If, to support them, he had occasional need to kill, well, one could not live a hard life without its penalties.

So the legend grew with the dead.

But also, with the dead, another factor grew, and this one was no folklore fostered by the buck-toothed gunman's kindness to old ladies or his charms for younger ones.

The responsible, quiet men of the Territory were talking in covert meeting places. These were the cowmen, the merchants, the townfolk of Lincoln, Sumner, Fort Stanton, and the other settlements of the land "Billito" had returned to haunt. Gradually their decisions drew together. A man was needed who knew the wolfish outlaw boy and was, at the same time, unafraid of him.

Finding the man took a bit more doing. That was because he was so close all the while that no one recognized him. It took a soft-voiced cattle buyer from the East, a stranger to that part of New Mexico, to nudge the final choice.

This took place when the buyer rode into town one afternoon in the company of famed local rancher John Chisum. A gentle fellow with a ready and engaging smile, the stranger stopped his horse and said to his companion, "Mr. Chisum, sir, who is that lean man yonder with the broad mustache? The tall one, with the ice-gray eyes, lounging there before that store, all easy and long-coiled like a cat?"

It was a peculiar description, and it caught at the mind of John Chisum.

He turned to see who it might be the pleasant buyer inquired after. When he did see, his eyes narrowed and he halted his own horse. "Friend," he said to the buyer, words low and tense with some excitement, "why do you ask?"

The eastern buyer smiled quickly. "Oh, it was nothing definite," he said. "A stray thought took me riding by. No more than that."

"What thought?" pressed Chisum, watching him.

"Why, only that I would not care to have that man after me." The buyer shrugged. "Now I suppose you think that's rather random, sir, if not outrightly foolish."

John Chisum shook his head, excitement growing. "Not at all, sir," he replied. "Wait here a moment, if you will. And take my thanks beforehand."

He turned his horse and rode over to the hitching rail of the general store. Halting the animal, he nodded to the owner of the place, the same long-coiled, catlike fellow described by the cattle buyer.

"Pat," he said, without amenities, "you are the man." Then, turning back, he joined the pale horseman waiting in the road. "Thank you, Mr. Asaph, sir," he said. "You have conferred a service here which none shall know officially, but one we local citizens may enter in the ledger of good luck, and thank the stars for sending you this way."

"I doubt the stars had much to do with it." Asaph smiled. "Nor luck the same. But if it humors you to think it so, then I am flattered. In my business, men are not often happy to be served my wares, much less to hail me on my way. A good day to you, Mr. Chisum, sir. I'll think about the cattle."

That was in 1880. The place was Fort Sumner, New Mexico. The man in front of the general store was Patrick Floyd Garrett, a lean expatriate Alabaman gone West to improve his fortunes in the post-war '60's, like a thousand others from the South before him. And what John Chisum meant by the blunt greeting just bestowed was that Pat Garrett was the man standing so close to history he had not been seen.

He was the man to hunt Billito down, to kill the killer.

For Billito and his coyotes of the chaparral, last earth was near. The Lincoln County War, so famed in song and myth, was fought, but it will not be waged again in this account. All who follow Billy's life know of that sordid struggle between Tunstall and McSween and the Murphy-Dolan faction for control, real and political, of Lincoln and its county. Billy fought for Tunstall as a gunman. They say he slew eight or nine or seven men, some say ten, but Asaph's record, whence this counting stems, says that the total number of the notches on his .41 that year when Garrett came to dog his trail stood at nineteen, two less than the years of his life.

And Asaph's record, cast ahead as only he could cast it, showed the final entry to precisely match that span, which then was twenty-one; a man for each year of his life.

There were thus two more men to die.

They must die quickly, too, for Billy's time to kill them ran now on a shortened rope, and tightening.

Asaph already had selected the men.

But first came Garrett on the trail and closing fast. He trapped Billy and four desperate companions in an abandoned ranch building at a place called Stinking Springs. Pat had an efficient posse with him, men who all knew why they were there. On the other hand Billy had often boasted that he would never be taken alive by living lawman, and Pat Garrett in particular. Thus when the Lincoln sheriff—he wore that star officially now—called aloud for Billy to come out, "hands high and walking slow," the gauntlet was down.

In the ancient house, Billy had his saddled mare, the noted gray La Chispa. Did he now spring on this splendid animal to carry out his claim, dash through the silent door onto the waiting riflemen, leap the mare and race her past the deadly guns of the quiet townsmen? Did this legend of the little folk of the *monte* ride thus through glory and gun smoke to freedom far and dear?

He did not: he first sent Charley Bowdre out to "test the wind and shooting light" of bullets meant for him. Bowdre, a man as tough and true as whang leather, walked out and took seven shots, all centered in his stomach, then still walked far enough to see Pat Garrett standing there and say, "Good morning, marshal, I am dead—good day."

After that came Billy. He showed up in the door, hands high, as told to do. The gray mare followed him, her head still high where his was not, her step still sure where his faltered with the white-lipped, sickly smile and whine, "I'm all done, Pat; don't shoot!"

The chase to corner him had been long and hard. It had carried beyond Las Vegas, and the posse's horses were all done. The result was to take the train and "ride the cars" back home, the captured outlaws, with their craven chief, trussed in iron cuffs but granted the freedom of the smoking car. At each exit stood a deputy with badge of office, his waiting Winchester.

Fearing that at Vegas the hostile mob of lookers-on might try to take the outlaw for their long-due own and "stretch him on the spot," the vigilance was doubled. A crowd did show up and did threaten. But Pat lounged to the platform with his thumb hooked in his vest, the coat turned back enough to show the walnut handle of the Colt worn low and buck-thong tied, and the crowd shrank away, its nerve failing.

From Vegas the train sped west to Santa Fe. From there, by secret ways, the renowned killer was borne to District Court to hear Judge Bristol admit the evidence, then, staring coldly from the bar, intone, "Swear the prisoner in."

The charge was murder, first degree, for the death of Sheriff William Brady in the Lincoln County War, wherein Billy had shot the lawman down, unseen, from behind a breast-high adobe wall. It was the act of a mad dog, now so judged.

"On the thirteenth day of May, eighteen eighty-one, at the county seat of Lincoln," droned the clerk, "you will be hanged as full deserved and as your many crimes insist

—not just this single one—and by the neck, and publicly, till you are dead."

That afternoon a visitor came unannounced to Billy's cell. It was Asaph.

"Ah, boy," he said, "think back to carefree days you knew when such as Jesse Evans rode your side and brave men like Segura risked their lives that you might win again and 'take it all,' as was your way.

"Why, in those days, no man stood taller in his mind than you. What happened in between to bring you to this lonely cell where ought of friends or visitors you have are those which come to gnaw at night, the bedbugs and the rats?"

"Cuss it all," scowled Billy, "lay off that singsong stuff! It gives a man the creeps. If you've ought to say of help, then say it. Elsewise, leave me be. Jailor!"

"Tut," said Asaph softly. "No need to make alarm. Not that I blame you, boy. The rope's a nasty thing to face. But I have come to help you, as you say. I've brought a gift of prophecy. Will you hear it out?"

He let a moment's silence intervene, black eyes peering into Billy's face. And Billy nodded, somehow afraid, and said he would hear the tale.

Asaph's thin lips parted.

"The last two men that I shall send to die beneath your guns will bear the names of Ollinger and Bell. I name them thus that you will know my tongue is true when the future brings your paths together, and the blood spills as I say it must."

"Stop!" cried Billy. "You're hexing me. That there's heathen mumbo jumbo. I don't need to set still for such daft talk. Jailor!"

But now a strange thing happened. Billy opened his mouth and the yell for the turnkey came out, but no sound was heard. The boy wheeled, white-faced, on Asaph.

"You are witching me, blast you. Let go my tongue."

Again he formed the shout, yet not one syllable of sound disturbed the eight-foot cell.

"If you wish to call it witchcraft," shrugged Asaph, not smiling but still gentle, "that is your affair. But you will listen to my augury all the same. When a man makes a bargain with me, he keeps it. You claim that rule yourself."

It was true. One of Billy's most frequent vows was that he would always do what he promised to do, keeping his word.

"Go on," he told Asaph wearily. "Mebbe there's something to your spell, after all. I ain't nothing to lose, nohow."

Asaph sat down upon the cell's rude cot. His dark glance lifted to the single narrow window, staring far away. The soft voice resumed its hypnotic murmur. Swiftly it foretold the fate which waited just beyond that cell for Billy Bonney. Almost before the listening boy realized it, the grim tale was done. Asaph's vibrant voice fell away. Billy shook his head. It seemed to him that he had merely dozed. Yet it was dark in the cell, and still as the grave, and Asaph was no longer there. Of a sudden, Billy was not sure of anything. Shakily, he lit the stub of candle he found tallowed to the window's sill. Seizing up the light, he cast its feeble ray about. The cell was empty.

No, not quite.

On the rude table by the cot a black book lay which had not been there before. Billy picked up the volume. He regarded it fearfully. He knew that it was Asaph's account book, and he believed that he knew the dread list which it contained. Or did it? And, if the list were there, did those two last names appear upon it in the manner Asaph had said?

No, it wasn't even Asaph's book. It was some prison Bible left there by the jailor as Billy drowsed. But no Bible had that snakelike skin for cover. The black book was actually coiling in Billy's hand. He could feel it move.

The boy opened the book, peering with the candle. His stomach turned cold. The two names were there:

Bell, J. W., deputy sheriff, Lincoln town.

Ollinger, Robert, deputy sheriff, Lincoln town.

Then, noted in a fresher ink which did not match the other, Billy saw a third and final name, and his voice grew low and whispery. "Oh, no," he said. "Not that name, not *there.*"

Asaph's prophecy was borne out with chilling speed. Billy, transferred to Lincoln town, was held in the old Murphy-Dolan store building. Assigned to guard him were deputies J. W. Bell and Bob Ollinger, as foretold by Asaph or, as Billy began to assure himself, by Asaph's ghost. For now the fugitive youth was believing what he wanted to believe. He had not seen Asaph since the jail cell visit, and the black book had vanished in some arcane fashion, meanwhile, and happily.

Accepting this as proof that he had dreamed the whole thing, the doomed prisoner at once began to dwell upon the problem of his escape. But when he arrived in Lincoln and was assigned deputies Bell and Ollinger as guards, he thought no more of dreams. The desperate light in his hazel-flecked eyes grew wilder still. All right, Asaph's augury was coming true. He, Billy, would play it as it seemed to go, and see what happened. He already had a foretold way in which to steal Bob Ollinger's sawed-off deadly scattergun. If that stolen shotgun part of the prophecy worked out and he got free, as the augury had said, then he would look up Asaph—or his ghost—and get the rest of the plan. All of it. Including that last name in the black book. The one that came past Ollinger's and Bell's, and written in a different, fresher ink.

But no. That last name was a mistake. It was an addition of Billy Bonney's imagination. Surely it was not Asaph's work to write it there.

Forcing the uneasy thought to fade, young Bonney shot down Bell and Ollinger with scant concern, knowing from Asaph's augury that he could not miss them with the stolen gun, nor they harm him in any way. He was free and standing laughing on the second floor balcony of the old store building, the smoke still curling from the muzzle of Ollinger's shotgun, when the first chill doubt assailed him.

Damnation! the augury was ended. He was free, just as it had said he would be free, but he was free in the middle of Lincoln, trapped on an upper balcony with an empty gun, still shackled with the leg irons upon which deputy Bell had counted so fatally to restrain the prisoner.

Curse the luck, where was Asaph now? Now, when a

man could use him? In the name of the Lord, why didn't he show up? The seconds, the minutes were ticking away. If his mother's strange friend were to make it in time, he would need to be wondrous quick. The minutes became five, ten. But shadowy Asaph did not appear, and Billy began to snarl like a cornered animal. The devil with Asaph—or his ghost, whichever. When the time came that Billy Bonney needed anybody, or anybody's spook, to show him what to do when guns and horses were to hand, then that would be the time to get the shakes.

Right now the game was his to play, and he would play it as he always had—to win.

Wheeling about, he left the balcony.

In Sheriff Garrett's deserted office room, where he had seized deputy Ollinger's shotgun, Billy now armed himself with a Winchester and two sixguns which he found there. Clanking down the hall and the stairway of Dolan's store in his leg irons, not looking down at his old friend deputy J. W. Bell as he was forced to step over his bullet-torn body, he made his way to the street. There was no attempt to hide himself. Billy the Kid had guns to hand again and feared no man in Lincoln. Not, at any rate, with Pat Garrett out of town.

From above, he had seen the man he wanted most, coming down Main toward the store. Now, as the fellow limped past, Billy shadowed out of the doorway and hailed him.

"Hello there, Mr. Geiss. Come in, come in, I've work for you."

Old Geiss, as he was called, was the German-born blacksmith of the town. A tough graybeard and strong as a salt cedar, he was old not only in years but in the ways to stay alive in that harsh climate. When informed that Billy Bonney needed shackles removed from his ankles and was willing to pay a bullet in the head to the blacksmith who refused the business, Old Geiss just nodded and replied, *"Ja, ja,"* and went on down the street to his shop and got his chisel.

Billy returned to the second floor of the store. There Old Geiss followed him and went to work on the leg irons while the Kid sat on the window sill of the front room talking with old friends below, who tarried in the street to inquire after his health and what they might be able to do for him. Billy's cool suggestion to these citizens was that they not try to leave town ahead of him, and, incredibly, they obeyed. The sly boy with his protruding overshot jaw, weak chin, bright eyes, and mad, quick grin had such a hold on the imaginations of the community that he was safe in Lincoln, even freed, and in fact and by the testimony of a dozen reliable witnesses he lingered two hours in the town, *after* old Geiss had cut him loose.

It was nearly twilight when at last he departed.

He had a good horse, the stout bay saddler of William Burt, a customer of Old Geiss. The blacksmith had just shod the animal, and he was full of oats and ready to run. So, too, was Billy Bonney. His trail, when last seen by the Lincolnites, lay toward Fort Stanton. The only actions of pursuit adopted by the cautious townfolk were the dispatches of private warnings to any enemy of "the Kid's" who might think him still safe in Dolan's Store. It was actually two full days before Pat Garrett could get back and gather a posse, the killing of the guards being on April 28, Garrett's start from Lincoln with the posse given as April 30.

The track, cold now on the barren dusty ground, ran due west four miles, then veered north to disappear in the direction of Las Tablas.

But the Kid was gone.

Fort Sumner, Cañaditas, Arenoso, and Tayban, and a hundred arcane cow-trail and sheep-track camps hid him well in those following weeks. Wherever he was reported, he was somewhere else by the time Garrett could arrive. Traps were laid, a score of positive sightings run down and dropped in disappointment. Nothing hard was learned. Billy had vanished.

His *pobrecitos*, his "poor ones," had welcomed him back and were telling no man with a star where Billito rode or slept.

But Billy was afraid.

Something had changed. He trusted no one now.

May, with its brief flowers, passed into June with its little rain. July sweltered next, its dust devils whirling toward August. Pete Maxwell's place, and Curington's, goatherds and cattle drovers, water tanks and railway switch tracks, lonely haunts and lonely men, saw much of him those fleeting final weeks.

And slowly the word crept back to Garrett: Billy, who knew all the range from Taos to Tucumcari, was circling back. He was going in a wide and wary swing out around the scene of his last kill. But like the wolf and coyote that he was, he could not help himself; he was heading back for Lincoln.

It was about this time that the sheriff had a letter. It came to him from a contact named Brazil, a rancher whose place had many times been used by Billy on the dodge.

"Our bird is back," the letter ran, "and covied up nearby. If you will meet me at Tayban, perhaps we'll flush him soon."

Although it was midday, and hot, Pat shivered.

Where could he find two men, just two men, who would side him walking up on that bird? Men he could trust to hold their fire until the flush, then not turn and run when the quarry broke covert? The outlaw had a thousand friends, or a hundred at the least. But the sheriff had to think the better part of the day to scrape up in his memory the names of two men he could depend on going after Billy. Even then, he had no certain way of knowing that these two might not, when told the nature of the game, get word to Billy and back out themselves. But brave Brazil had chanced sure death to write the note. Garrett must sound out his aides.

First was John Poe. Poe was a good man, hard to bluff, an employee of the Stockmen's Association, experienced in trailing elusive prey. Poe would not turn tail or belly-up when called. He would stand and deliver. All right, then, Poe was one.

Next, T. K. McKinney. Tom McKinney was likewise a working gun. He had been where the owl hooted and come back from there. He would do.

Garrett contacted them late at night on the roadside beyond Lincoln's lights. "Now, boys," he said, the careful words slow-spaced, "this is a chancy trip. You know the

Kid. If either one of you wants out, just say the word and travel. Stay with me and we ride tonight for Roswell. That's where he is."

Both listeners nodded and neck-reined their horses to side Pat Garrett's. "Let's go," they said as one.

The three men rode away, Garrett tall and proud between his deputies. A mackerel sky striped the moon's white face, shadowing the sage at roadside. Out of the gloom thus made rode a fourth horseman, a stranger on a pale mount.

Halting the gaunt animal, Asaph stared off after the Lincoln sheriff and his hard-eyed henchmen.

There went three good men, the kind that Asaph shunned for lack of profit in the breed. To such as them the law meant something, enough that they would die for it. To young Bonney it meant nothing, not the law, nor the lawmen riding out in its just name. Of all the trashy lies men told in the behalf of Billy, none was so false, so ludicrous, so bald of proof as that which declared the buck-toothed weasel to be the good pal and boon companion of Pat Garrett, or the other way around.

Pat Garrett knew the Kid, and nothing more.

Past that, the two were scarcely of the same race. Pat was a man. Billy of the crooked grin, the protruding fangs, the dirty freckles, and the wild eyes, now green, now blue now gray, but always wild—why, Billy was a boy, no more, and rotten to the sapwood of his spine.

At no time since he knifed the drunken man in Dyer's place had he been anything but the outlaw thief and bandit chief who cheated, stole, laughed, lied, cringed, and killed, for money.

Yet Asaph, watching his executioners ride forth into that moon-streaked July night, felt a moment's strange compassion for the boy. He detested him, yes. But what rose in the stranger's mind, as now he knew the end drew near, was pity. Not disdain, not contempt, not censure. Just simple pity.

What a wonder it was that a bright boy like this, true to himself and to others once, could have fallen so that he be tracked and trailed and stalked like an animal gone mad, which must be cornered and destroyed because it now struck out in senseless viciousness at all who passed it, or drew near, or even took its name in vain, or called in sympathy for it to come forth.

Who had helped him on this way? Anyone? Aspah, perhaps?

No, it wasn't Asaph, it wasn't anyone, it was Billy.

Men are born to be bad, and men are born to be good. In the meanwhile, neither saints nor sinners are made by good or bad advice. It takes two to make a partnership in crime: one to propose, one to listen. After that, what matter if, from mercy or whatever aim, one guides the other so to expedite the thing and have it over with?

"Come, bony one," said Asaph softly to the horse. "We must not fall too far behind, who would be there when needed most. The track turns north again before Roswell, and moonrise, two weeks hence. Fort Sumner is the way, I think. What was that name again? Tayban Arroyo? Why waste time with Garrett and his friends? We'll simply go and wait."

In Tayban Arroyo, on the thirteenth night from Lincoln, July of 1881, the wind lay still, the canyon dark. With John Poe and Tom McKinney, Garrett waited in the ghostly rocks for their contact man, Brazil. But the Mexican had fled. Fear had found him before they did. He was gone, afraid to fail Billito, or have his people know his part in bringing Garrett there.

Next day Poe, a stranger to those parts, was sent by Pat into Fort Sumner to "nose around" and see what he might learn of Billy's latest boast. He was to do nothing but lounge about the town square—the listening post—and let come to his attention what might. He was to return that night with his report, meeting Garrett and McKinney at Punta Glorieta, a local landmark. Meanwhile they, too, would scout around.

Poe came to the meeting ground at moonrise, on time. He waited perhaps five minutes before hearing from the river bed below the bark of a fox. It was their agreed recognition signal. If the track had been found hot, three barks by the finder. If cold, but a single yelp. If danger threatened the meeting place, if either party to it had been followed, two sharp yaps. Now John Poe waited anxiously for any sound past that first thin yip. And he got it. After a pause, two more yapping barks. *Three!* The hunt was on.

Down into the river bed he went. The three lawmen conferred swiftly. McKinney and Garrett had gotten the same information from the countryside—from a lone cowboy here, a tight-lipped ranch owner there—that Poe had gathered in the town. They had their fox run down.

He was at Pete Maxwell's place.

"All right," said Pat, "let's go. You know Pete's layout, Tom. We'll go in through the orchard behind the house. Poe can cover us."

"Yup," said Tom McKinney, grinning dry and quick. "He can cover us either way: with gun or spade."

"I'll promise it," said stolid Poe. "Let's ramble."

Asaph sat on a rock in the moonlight above the river bed, the highest he could sit at Punta Glorieta and still hear, with that ear of his so much keener than it ought to be, what passed of conversation among the three lean riders from Lincoln.

When they had gone, Pat Garrett again in the lead, his hired guns flanking him, McKinney left and Poe right, Asaph smiled.

"Do you see," he said to the pale horse, standing reins trailing beside the rock, "how true they run to our directions? Would they ever think to ask one another *who* gave each the information that the other brought? Would they wonder how remarkable it was that they could hear the same story in Sumner as in the sagebrush?"

The horse nickered in agreement.

"No," said Asaph, "they would not compare the data. Had they, now, would it not bemuse them to understand that stout Poe met the same slim stranger in Fort Sumner as McKinney and good Pat encountered on the cow trail and at the ranchhouse out here in the emptiness of deer trails and coyote dens? Of course. Yet would it not bemuse them more, should they learn that, five days back, the same slim stranger and his bony horse met Billy Bonney on the owlhoot road and told him where to go? Ah, now, how very small their minds. Do they all imagine that the words 'Pete Maxwell's place' popped all unaided into their heads, and in a perfect sequence of suggestion, so as to bring all four into conjunction at that spot *in one same hour?"*

Asaph laughed softly.

"Strange," he said, "and just a little sad."

He sat yet another moment, looking off through the moonlight to where the three figures of the distant horsemen dwindled on the trail to Maxwell's ranch.

His voice took on that rhythmic cadence which Billy had cursed as "singsong" but which another ear might have labeled as a form of speech far older than any man then living.

"I set them on his trail," he said, "and yet I cannot say I feel well for it. Indeed, I bring them to him haltingly. Admire him, I do not. Who cherishes the coward, thief, and murderer? Not I, despite the things men say of me. It is that Billy has within him elements of all the sorrow and despair of man, wrapped in a cloak of happy dignity.

"Where he has killed, even lurking in the shadows or behind some leafy wall, he has known remorse, or call it conscience, if you will; he still would stand above the corpse and murmur down, 'Now, blast it, Bob—or Joe or Jim or Jack—I'm sorry as all glory!'

"What he stole of horse or gun or food, or even of some maiden's virtue, he always sent a message back avowing full repayment. What matters it, as heroes go, that never in all that time of vowing did he once make good his word?

"When he lied, he lied to good effect, such as to save his life or sacrifice that of another, perhaps that of some friend who loved him as a brother, or a son, and would have died for him, unasked, and so no real treason done.

"Ah, thus the charm he's borne. It has been, withal, remarkable. Sheltering him from winter's wind and summer's sun, alike, for twenty years, and thus far part of twenty-one. Which part now is run, alas, leaving Billy and his charm undone."

The bony white horse whickered inquiringly, expecting more. But Asaph had finished.

He arose from the rock. "Do you know," he said, the

soft laugh falling once more, "that I have so engrossed myself with his past that I've forgotten where he's going now! Another moment, yet, patient friend."

He took from inside his coat the slender black book and, holding it to the moonlight, squinted frowningly.

"Ah, yes," he said, the smile restored. *"Pete Maxwell's place."* Then added, softer still, and mounting up with haste, "Come on, old ghost, it's all been said: let's go."

"This will do."

Pat Garrett reined his pony in.

"We'll go in from here afoot," he continued. "This old orchard's our best cover. Tie your horses. We don't want them wandering."

"It's funny Pete would put him up," said McKinney.

"Not funny to Pete, likely," added Poe. "The Kid no doubt asked for board and bed, Mex-style, with his gun or knife."

"Walk up soft, now," said Pat Garrett. "Hold your pistols cocked. Don't shoot until you hear me say, 'That's him.' "

They went through the orchard trees, gnarled and dim-seen, the moon having gone behind cloud. They could see the main house of the Maxwell ranch ahead. There was no light in it. There was not, either, any sound of human voices from the main building. But a square Mexican adobe hut lay between them and the ranchhouse, and from that source they did hear voices coming. The tongue was Spanish. Neither Garrett nor Poe nor McKinney recognized any of the speakers, of which they made out three, at least, for number.

This failure to identify one of the voices put the sure lie to the legend claiming Pat and Billy to be friends.

For the third speaker was the Kid.

Garrett, had the myth been true of his great fondness for young Bonney, would certainly have known that buck-toothed lisp in any tongue. But he did not know Bonney that well, and he did not recognize his voice that night, nor did his two companions, Poe and McKinney.

But now Garrett paused, hearing those soft tongues of the *monte* from the hut. He saw three shadows squatting near an adobe wall, close by the door of the small house. These must be Maxwell's Mexican hands, his *mozos*, servants, something. One of them arose and, yawning, said he was going to bed. He went into the adobe, lifting its cowhide door flap and disappearing from view. The watchers saw a lamp turn up inside the hut.

Then they did a strange thing.

The man who had gone in to retire was the one with the lisp, the buck-toothed boy, Billy Bonney. Yet the lawmen still did not know him, still turned away from that small house, where there were both light and voices, and went on to the big house where neither lamp nor sound was evidenced.

Why?

Did Garrett, when he signaled with his hand in silence for Poe and McKinney to follow him, know something he had not told his deputies? Was there a trap within the trap?

Did he leave Billy in that hut on purpose?

Did he go on to the main house knowing *something?*

If not, why had he failed to order the surround sprung on the outlaw at the hut, where they had him dead to rights and "caught cold" in a one-roomed shack with no escape?

The legend goes that Billy grew hungry after deciding to bed down, that he got up and told his Mexican host, Maxwell's hired hand, that he was going "Down to Pete's and get a slice of beef" from a fresh quarter he knew to be hanging on the ranch porch. This was Garrett's story, told in retrospect and after the grim fact of Billy's "taking."

It did not match with Asaph's.

The soft-voiced stranger knew better. He stood in the same shadows of that adobe hut which sheltered the crouching lawmen from Lincoln. And he stood in those shadows *after* those lawmen had crept away, on down to the main ranchhouse, and were ready there. *Then* he heard what truly passed between Billy and the Mexican hand: it was not Billy Bonney who said, "I am going down to Pete's," but the Mexican servant of Maxwell who ordered—no, who suggested to the outlaw, "Billito, *amigo*, Pete he says he wants to see you; go down to the house."

Did Billy Bonney *go*, or was he *sent?*

Asaph knew but never told. He saw no need to say that Garrett lied. A lawman never tells all that he knows, or, if he does, he soon finds himself the victim of his own honesty. Pat Garrett was a brave man, good and true. He went where his sheriff's star directed him, needing no testament from such as Asaph, in the going.

At the main house, Pat stationed his two henchmen in an ambush of the covered porch, twenty feet from Maxwell's room.

Maxwell lay on his bed, but wide awake. He also knew something.

When Garrett had first seen Billy that night, when the Kid went unrecognized at the Mexican's hut, Billy had worn his hat, his boots, his guns. His pony had been staked nearby and saddled. Would that have been the posture of a welcomed man at ease among companions he could trust, a man who knew no hint of the deadly danger around him, a man who had never been taken by the law, unless through traitors softened with the touch of silver on the palm?

Why then the change? Why the sudden decision to go in the adobe and undress, and then, half-clad, to come down through the dark to Maxwell's house, unarmed, save for the butcher knife borrowed from "Pablo" to take his cut of beef?

For fools this story may suffice.

Men with harder minds will say that Billy was betrayed —that someone took a bribe.

Yet Garrett never spoke of bounty paid. Nor did Maxwell leave a memoir of his price. Neither did the Mexican, sly Pablo, advertise his pay among his people.

The trap, no matter, was ready-set.

In through the open window of Pete's room, Pat Garrett went like a mountain cat's shadow. Pete saw him come and still made no move to leave his bed. Getting behind the bed, putting his lean back to the protection of the thick adobe wall, Garrett waved his pistol, spoke fast and low.

"Where is he?"

Maxwell was a big man, and tough with years. In the daylight he feared few others. But this was different. They were not alone in that room, both knew it.

"Where is Billy?" repeated Pat, his tension growing with the bedroom's eerie midnight quiet.

"I don't know," whispered Pete. "He's here, but I don't know where."

"Maxwell, I was told you'd have him *here*."

"I will, I will, just wait."

With Maxwell's muttered promise, Garrett stiffened. Outside, the sound of muffled footsteps and a cheery whistle, known by ear to Pat Garrett, approached the porch.

"That's him!" hissed Garrett.

Again outside, the sound now of muffled voices, Billy's voice asking of the evening from Pat's two guards, Poe and McKinney playing their parts well, answering him in the Spanish language of the land, posing as passers-through much like himself.

Now the whistle resumed. Less cheery now, guarded, showing more breath than melody. The bootless footsteps crossed the porch, entered the main *sala* or front room, glided down the short hallway to Maxwell's door, pausing there.

Garrett tensed and raised his gun.

In the doorway the small figure seemed slight, almost boyish. The light behind it was growing, as the moon slithered out from underneath its cloud. There could be no doubt of the fact that the newcomer was unarmed as to any gun. The question was as to whether he even still carried the butcher knife. Maxwell, rigid on the bed, saw nothing in his hands.

But he knew the graceful boylike form, and so did Pat.

"Pedro," called Billy thinly, whisper high with some unease. *¿Quiénes son estos hombres afuera?* Who are those men outside?"

Pete, fearing to be shot by Garrett, said nothing.

Billy slid on into the room, still looking back over his shoulder toward the porch. "Pete!" he repeated sharply. "Answer me. Who's outside there? Those two men on the porch? Answer me!" His lisp was snakelike now, the alarm in it high and wild.

He came to the side of Pete's bed, bending over it. It was then his eyes made out the tall shadow standing beyond that bed, against the wall. He straightened.

"¿Quién es?" he whispered fearfully. "Who is it?" The tall shadow not replying, he turned again in panic to Pete Maxwell. "Pete, in God's name, who is there?"

This time his answer was not silence.

Another shadow came into the room, spoke at his elbow.

"It is I," said Asaph softly. *"It is I who awaits you here,"* and the thunder of Pat Garrett's gun broke loose.

Two times its lightning lanced the gloom.

The first shot, the range so close the flaring ball of powder gases ignited Billy's shirt and burned the flesh beneath, went in directly over the heart. It severed the main aorta and both its branches, rupturing out the blood and the life alike. The only sound that Billy made which was remembered by his human witnesses in that darkened room, was a simple, gasping, "Oh—!" Then Garrett's second shot, missing wide, screamed off the wall and brought the final silence in behind it, thick and hushed.

Oh, *what?* had Billy meant to say, in dying?

Oh, Lord? Oh, shame? Oh, curse the fates which lured me here?

Only Asaph knew, and he would not say because the words held in them that name which made him pale: they were "Oh, God, please help me, Mother!"

But let the legend have its way. He died without another sound, it says, except to struggle once or twice and "strangle some," as Garrett put it. This ending would suffice for Asaph. When he had touched a man and said to come, that man went with him. He cared not for legends or for lies, or folklore, left behind. He was Asaph the Gatherer. When he had harvested the grain, the chaff might blow forever where it would.

Thus he took Billy Bonney's hand and they, not hurried then, went out of that smoke-stinking room and mounted up on Asaph's pale horse, waiting beyond the lamplight now flooding Maxwell's ranch, its yard, and all around.

They rode, not swiftly, Billy thought, yet soon were halted far away. Here, Asaph, looking back toward the ranch, asked Billy if he wanted the answer to his whispered *"¿Quién es?"* in that dark room before the thunder of the gun. Would he wish now to know the name of the gunman who had killed him, and the names of those who waited on the porch to back him up? Or would he rather wait to ask Eternity?

Billy thought it through. He was never the one to rush his play before the hand was dealt. He glanced at Asaph, blue eyes unafraid but filled with all those nameless things which haunt the eyes of men who look at that companion.

At last he answered, high voice firm, sturdy shoulders squared. "No, friend," he said. "That *'¿quién es?'* was not for them, but you. I saw you all the time. I knew you were there. I only spoke to hear you say your name, and call mine after it."

"And now?" said Asaph, waiting still.

"Now?" said Billy, grinning wide. "Why the devil, pal; now let's go. You know the way, and so do I!"

Asaph nodded, and they traveled on to that far bourn from which no man returns. But as they went he noted that his comrade's step was light, his head unbent, the laughter that had been his life still ringing softly back across their footprints through the dust of Time.

BANDITS OF TEHUANTLTUX

"Gomez," inquired Pato, "why don't you come along with us and be bandits?"

Gomez swabbed the bar top. He studied the fly resting on the considerable bulb of his nose.

"Me," he said, "a bandit?"

"Why not? Among the three of us, we have it all. I supply the quality. Perro brings his doglike devotion. And you, Gomez—ah, you have the—"

"I have the gun," interrupted the proprietor of the Golondrina. "You do not fool me, Pato. I am a shrewd man."

"Exactamente," surrendered the other.

"And I own this cantina, also," declared Gomez.

"Of course. A man of property as well as of craft."

From the darkest corner of the earthen-floored room, the slow-minded youth who was called Perro nodded earnestly.

"A true thing, *compañeros,"* he called. "Very true."

Pato ignored him, watching Gomez. "Look patrón," he said, "come with me to the door here. *Por favor*."

Gomez laid aside his sour bar rag. He did not, however, disturb the fly on his nose. The small creature was known to him and not a bad fellow, either.

At the door he squinted his eyes to the bright sunlight. "Well," he said to Pato, "which way will you have me look?"

"At the river," directed the other. "What do you see?"

"Water," answered Gomez.

"Very good. What else?"

"Sand."

"Also good. What else?"

"A small city on the other side of the channel."

"Excellent. Do you recognize this small city?"

"Most certainly. I was born there. That is Tehuantltux. I once owned a fine cantina in that city."

"Yes, and what of the fine cantina? Where is it now?"

"Why, it is here, where we stand in it, on this side of the river, where it has been ever since the big flood."

"Precisely, patrón. Now what else do you see of Tehuantltux on this side of the river, other than your fine cantina?"

"Sand and water, that is all."

"And the good blue sky, eh, Gomez? All the rest is gone with the flood. The cantina is cut off from Tehuantltux, no? Do I say a true thing?"

At this, Perro, the giant boy with the mind of the newest baby, bobbed his shaggy head and cried out, "A true thing, *compañeros*. Very true."

The mindless youth had trotted up from his dark corner in the cantina to join them in the sunlight of the open doorway. Pato, who had found him abandoned to die in a Tehuantltux trash can as a newborn child and had reared and trained him precisely as any kind-hearted wayfarer would rear and train the orphaned stray of such an origin—as a servant, a companion, a faithful pet—Pato now gave Perro a kindly pat on the head. "Go back into your corner and lie down," he said. And Perro, far larger than any man in Tehuantltux even if but fourteen years of age, barked obediently and trotted back into the cantina. Turning around three times, he lay down under his table, the last one in the corner, and ever doglike, began to pant contentedly.

"He is a good fellow," said Pato. "Now then, Gomez, do we agree I speak the truth? There has not been one human customer in the Golondrina since the flood washed away the bridge?"

"You have been in it," pointed out Gomez.

"I am not a customer; I am a friend."

"Well, Perro, then."

"Perro is scarcely human, much less a customer."

"He drinks my wine."

"But he does not pay for it. Does a dog offer money for the water in the gutter of the street?"

"You call my place a gutter?"

"Never. I only say that Perro does not pay."

"Perro is poor. He has no money. Why should he pay?"

"If he has no money, why should you give him wine?"

"He is my friend."

"And what am I?"

"You are my friend, too, Pato; you don't pay me for the wine, either."

"Bah, you're impossible!"

"*Sí*, but I have the gun, eh?"

"The gun?"

"Yes, to be bandits with."

"Oh, of course, that gun. All right, now, shut up. No more fooling, Gomez. Do you want to go with us and be bandits, or don't you? Forget the gun."

Gomez went back to his bar. He began slapping the sour rag against the dark wet wood. The fly got up and buzzed away from its rest on his nose. There was a displeased vibrancy to its departure. Gomez took alarm.

"A thousand pardons, Guillermo!" he called out after the fly. "Come back, I have something for you." He reached beneath the bar and brought forth a moldy piece of cheddar, a very ancient, very important, wedge of cheese. "Have a bit of the best, *amigo*," he added apologetically. "It's from the interior. Made from the milk of mountain cattle."

The fly wheeled about, banking sharply in its flight. It returned, settled upon the cheese, fell to feeding greedily. "Remarkable," observed Pato. "Consider the order of its intelligence. The brain must be no larger than the egg of a flea, yet it hears you and responds. You are a gifted man, jefe. And you thought I sought after you only for the gun!"

A glow, almost, suffused the round, sweat-beaded face of Porfirio Gomez.

"Jefe." He sighed. "You call me that, Pato? Your leader?"

"Forgive it, old friend," pleaded the other. "It slipped out. It is the natural way in which you take command, in which you issue an order. Why, that fly turned about as though it had been sent for by Zapata or Juárez, even Villa, perhaps. I don't see how you do it, Porfirio."

"De nada. It's really nothing, Pato. You know my grandfather was with Santa Ana at the Alamo. A *coronel* of the Cavalry. It is in the blood."

"The Alamo, you say? I always thought your grandfather was at Goliad."

"What? My grandfather at Goliad? Never. Only cowards were there. We lost, didn't we?"

"But brave men sometimes lose, Gomez. That's a fact."

"No, no, you don't trick me. My gradufather was at the Alamo, where we won."

"If you say so." Pato could be gracious. "How about being bandits with us, *Coronel?* It is all the more important to have you as our leader now. I hadn't known about the grandfather at the Alamo. All the time I thought he was at Goliad. *¿Qué tal?"*

Gomez glowed a bit more.

This idea of being bandits had its attractions.

The Golondrina was a splendid cantina, but it would never make another peso so long as the river had split it away from the town of Tehuantltux and no move was made to rebuild the bridge which Pato had said lay now upon the beach at Escopal.

But outlawry had its risk, too.

"I don't know." He was worried. "Killing people and taking their money can be hard work. Sometimes they object to being robbed or shot. Even a *pistolero* must take care."

"Man must work," said Pato sternly. "God put him here to toil. Besides, a danger exists in all callings. Moreover, a good bandit does much for the community. He takes from the rich and gives to the poor. Mother Church welcomes him. He prays little and lies at confession but puts much gold in the plate when it is passed. Women also seek after him. He is kind to little children. Dogs love him. I would not want to say that being bandits is all hard work, *amigo*. One must think of the other benefits, as well."

Gomez licked his lips. "Where are you going to be bandits?" he asked.

"Up there." Pato flung a lank arm toward the interior plateau. "On the high plain, out of this rotten jungle swamp and desert of hot sand where we dwell. Up in that good clean air, that's where all the *bandidos* are, and all of the horses, and the gold, and the women."

"Ah, those women!" breathed Gomez. *"¡Santísima!"*

"You will do it, then, Porfirio? You will go with us?"

"Well, I don't know, Pato."

"Jefe, we need you. You are the *Pistolero*. The Leader. The Chief. What are Perro and Pato without you?"

"Hungry," said Gomez.

"What?" Pato was stunned. "You begrudge us the food we accept from you? For shame!"

Gomez spread his pudgy hands. "No, no, it is not that I resent feeding you these twelve years, Pato," he said. "In truth, what would the Golondrina have been without you and Perro and all of those tricks you have taught him to do and which he performs better than any real dog? Such as fetching the thrown stick, sitting up and begging, rolling over and playing dead, jumping through the hoop. All of these things have been very good for business. I would never say you two old comrades had not earned your food. My idea was solely that, but for Gomez, you both would have starved."

Pato, hard against the merciless viewpoint of the *capitalista*, surrended.

"Exactly my position," he explained. "If you don't go with us to be bandits, we will die of cold and hunger upon some lonely mountain road up there. But with Gomez the Bandit to lead us, ah! the gold, the women, the rich life!"

"Gomez the Bandit," muttered the proprietor of the Golondrina. "It does have a ring to it."

"But not enough of a ring, jefe. Try El Tigre."

"Me?" The voice of Porfirio Gomez grew weak with emotion. "Do you mean that I shall be El Tigre?"

"Why not? Don't you like the sound of the Tiger of Tehuantltux?"

"The Tiger of Tehuantltux," breathed Gomez.

"There is a condition," warned Pato. "Perro and myself, we shall call you simply Tiger. But that is strictly as a privilege of old friends."

"I would insist on it." The Tiger of Tehuantltux blushed.

"Glory to God," announced Pato, raising his arms as he had seen the padre do on somber occasions. "Bless this fearless leader and his humble followers, O Father. Guide us on our mission of mercy to relieve the poor. In the name of the Father, the Son, and the Holy Goat, Amen."

"Ghost! Ghost!" cried Gomez in alarm. "The Holy Ghost!"

"Ghost, Goat, what difference?" demanded Pato. "Religion is like love; it is in the heart of the individual."

From the gloom beyond the reach of the oil lamp on the bar, the flat-toned voice of the third of the bandits of Tehuantltux echoed its high refrain. "A true thing, *compañeros*, very true."

"You see?" said Pato to Gomez. "Even Perro understands the nobility of your commitment, jefe." Then, before Gomez might deny the connection, he began to whistle and clap his hands and call out excitedly. "*Hai* Perro! Come on, boy, let's go. Good boy, good boy."

Perro, aroused, bounded out of his dark corner and ran around in circles barking and jumping up on Pato.

"Down! Down! shouted the latter, defending himself. "There, that's a good fellow. We'll be ready in a moment."

Behind the bar, Gomez was removing his apron.

"Let's see now," he said, observing himself. "I have put on my sombrero, there is my serape waiting, here is the gun in my hand ready to be belted on—have I forgotten something? Oh, yes, to blow out the lamp." He puffed at the lamp, plunging the Golondrina into still more Stygian shadow. "Now, anything else? Ah, yes, Guillermo. Forgive me, small friend," he said, waving into the general darkness. "Where are you? Come on. No hiding. We are in a hurry."

The fly buzzed in out of the winy gloom, settled in its accustomed place upon the Gomez nose, and commenced to brush its hind legs contentedly. "You have your Perro" —the proprietor smirked—"I have my Guillermo. Let us proceed."

Regretfully, Pato shook his head.

"No, jefe," he said. "Up in the cold climate of the plateau Guillermo will not survive. One cold night and—poof!"

Gomez crossed his eyes, focusing them upon the end of his nose and upon Guillermo.

"Pato is right," he told the fly. "You will have to stay here. Eat the good cheese and get a lot of rest. We won't be away forever."

The fly glared at him with its thousand eyes. It buzzed in a peremptory high tone, then flew over to the cheese.

"I don't know," worried Gomez. "Guillermo is not pleased."

"Look," said Pato hurriedly, "permit me to talk with him. We will enjoy a less emotional relationship. He has his place in society. We are all brothers. I know that I can persuade him, make him see the wrongness and futliity of his anger."

"Oh, thank you, Pato. You always understand these things."

"But of course, jefe. Take Perro and wait outside."

Gomez whistled to the hulking Perro and departed. Pato turned to the fly.

"Guillermo," he said, "listen. In the nature of things a man must do many acts which may not appear charitable to those who receive the benison. Such a better thing than you are able to comprehend now comes to you."

Pato picked up the piece of bar chedder upon which Guillermo perched attentively. He stubbed the cheese against the adobe wall, embedding the fly in the rubbery curd. He then went outside and tossed the cheese to Perro, saying, "Catch!"

Perro opened his large mouth and snapped up the tidbit.

"Good boy." Pato nodded.

"You were able to convince Guillermo?" asked Gomez anxiously.

"Absolutely."

"That is nice. He truly wished to go with us. I could see it in all of his eyes."

"Look at it this way, *compadre*," suggested Pato philosophically. "In a sense you are not leaving him behind. Believe it." He straightened, turning for the river. "Trust in Pato. Forget the Golondrina. Forward, march; we are off to the interior."

Gomez and Perro fell in behind him. Gomez was no longer worried. Perro ran in and out of the bottomland brush, flushing cactus sparrows and barking happily. The sky was cerulean blue. The river sparkled in the sunlight. The dust was soft and warm to the bare foot. Everything smelled of summer and success. It was a fine day to begin being bandits.

They followed the river path. Pato, an educated person, was aware that water flowed downhill. He reasoned from this that they had but to follow upward the gentle current of the Rio Zorrillo to reach the highlands. Being persons of no education, Gomez and Perro found themselves fortunate to be in such learned company. But not even Pato was invulnerable. They had not gone far when he stopped in his tracks.

"*¡Pardiez!*" he cried, striking himself in the forehead. "Do you know what I have forgotten? The horses!"

"What horses?" Gomez blinked.

"What horses!" stormed Pato. "Did Pancho Villa walk to fame and fortune? Did you ever see a statue of Zapata dismounted? We must have horses!"

"*Sí*, but how can we buy them? We have no *dinero*."

"*Buy* our horses? God's name, Gomez! Since when did bandits buy anything? *¡Por Dios!* We steal them."

"*Steal?*" Porfirio Gomez grew pale. "You must be crazy, *hombre*. I never stole anything in my life."

Pato flinched visibly. "What do you think it is that bandits do, *amigo?*" he asked. "Borrow?"

"Bandits rob. Anyone knows that."

"Yes, of course. I thought only to be sure you had the distinction clearly in your mind, jefe."

"I do. Now how about the horses, Pato?"

"We will rob them."

"Good. Where?"

"Up the river."

"Up the river is only old Esteban Miraflor. He has no horses, only burros."

"We shall see," said Pato. "If he cannot produce mounts, we may need to kill him. Have the gun ready. But right at this time let us go into the river and get cool. Careful with the gun. Don't get it wet. Don't get the bullet wet either. We don't want it to misfire when we must shoot somebody."

"Yes," said Gomez. "With but a single bullet, one cannot be too careful. I will place it here upon my *pantalones*."

"Perhaps I had better take the gun; you keep the bullet."

"No, no!" Gomez was not to be so easily taken. "I am the *pistolero!*" He backed away, sheltering the weapon.

Big Perro raised a hand the size of a Yucatán ham. "A true thing, *compañeros*," he said. "Very true."

"All right. Who cares anyway? Ready for the water, *amigos?*" Pato, the realist, did not strain at gnats. "Here we go."

"Wait!" It was now Porfirio Gomez who held up the restraining hand. "I just thought of something. This bullet won't fire anyway. I tried it last summer. It just went 'clunk.' Now what are we going to do if we have to shoot old Miraflor?"

Pato waved the point airily aside. "Jefe," he said, "you are the Leader. You don't ask questions, you give orders. Come on, now. Everybody into the water. *¡Hai!*"

Gomez still hesitated, frowning. But Perro gave a happy bark, dropped to all fours, and dashed into the shallows of the stream. Pato, waddling like the duck for which he was named, followed the huge simpleton into the water. Gomez lost his frown. He let the *pantalones* fall the rest of the way. The rusted gun and the verdigrised bullet would wait. So would Old Man Miraflor and his burros and the whole business of being bandits. Pato was right. The important thing just then was that cool green river.

"Look out, *amigos!*" he shouted. "Here comes the Tiger of Tehuantltux!"

Crouched in the thicket which barricaded the river-bottom rancho of Esteban Miraflor, the three desperadoes took pause.

Esteban's place was expansive, perhaps as much as an entire acre of cleared ground in its full sweep. Opulence was everywhere. There stood a splendid woodpile containing enough cut wood for at least two meals ahead. Four pigs could be counted, and eleven chickens, eight of which seemed well. There were also a turkey hen and two lame geese, and a milk-goat with a mattered udder. But it was not this wealth of producing livestock which drew the professional eye of the hidden outlaws.

"Aha!" breathed Pato. "What did I tell you? Look at those two beauties over there in the corral! With such fleet steeds beneath us we can laugh at any *rurales* or *federalistas* in the land. Nothing in all of Mexico can match us, not even the swiftest wind. Which one do you choose, jefe?"

Gomez scowled. "Of those twins of despair?" he said. "What difference?"

"Shhh! Careful. Quiet. They might hear you. Such highborn creatures are all spirit. They have the nerves of lions, the natures of fine beautiful women. Chargers like those must be treated as royalty. Come, my leader. Which will you have of them? The black Spanish Majorca jack or the brown clean-limbed Sonora jennet?"

"Pato," said Gomez, "you are afflicted. Those are the two burros of Old Man Miraflor. He calls the one Chapultepec and the other Bustamante."

There was despair in the look which Pato flung him. But there was in the look compassion as well. And some awe.

"The mark of the true hidalgo," he murmured. "He sees the blood and breeding, yet to make his lesser-born companions not to feel ill at ease, he professes to be blind."

"Nevertheless"—Gomez nodded pleasantly—"I still know those two jackasses. Hello there, Bustamante. Greetings, Chapultepec. It is I, your old friend, Gomez the Bandit."

With the salutation, he stepped out of the brush before

Pato could seize him. It was too late in any event. The sound of his voice had carried to the adobe hovel from which Old Miraflor surveyed his hectares of empire on the banks of the Rio Zorrillo, rousing the ancient landowner.

"Here! Here!" yelled the old man, tottering out of the door. "What is this? Company? Someone comes to visit Esteban Miraflor and goes unwelcomed to his house?"

He stopped short of a curled-up and soundly sleeping mongrel which lay across the door path.

"Get up, you misbegotten rascal!" he screeched at the dog, kicking the beast repeatedly in the ribs and rump. "Strangers and thieves could rob and kill me and you never open an eye. *¡Arriba, arriba!* Do something!"

The bewildered dog, thus set upon, leaped to its feet and rushed about, looking for the enemy or for anything. He saw Gomez just as Pato snatched him back into the thicket. With a brave snarl, he charged the covert.

"Now see what you have done, you fat fool!" cried Pato. "Here comes the dog. We are discovered."

"Well," said Gomez, not alarmed, "I cannot imagine what the old man means by setting his dog on us, but if he is going to do that, then we must set our dog loose, also. Go and get them, Perro. I command you."

Perro needed little urging. With a mighty growl he charged out of the thicket. Esteban's cur gave a heart-rending squall of pure fear, turned tail, and raced back toward its peering master. When the latter's rheumy vision made out the sight of huge Perro running at him upon all fours, the old man fell into a foot race with his dog for the sanctuary of the single acacia tree planted in the ranch-yard. Master and brute scrambled up the thorny stem as one and ended huddled together in the higher branches, Perro leaping and baying at the bole of the acacia beneath them.

Seeing the quarry treed, Pato and Gomez quit the thicket and came lumbering up to the scrawny acacia.

"Who is that down there?" called the old man. "And what is that monster you have set upon me and my brave dog? Is it human? Speak up, speak up, or I shall loose my fierce dog upon you again."

"Don't do that, Esteban." Gomez waved. "Save the

trouble. It is only I, Porfirio Gomez, the Tiger of Tehuantltux. I and my faithful *teniente*, Pato the Duck. This is our friend Perro the Dog who leaps at the bole of your nice tree."

"You?" shouted the ancient one, enraged. "Fat Gomez from the Golondrina? What is the meaning of this outrage? What do you want of Miraflor? Be quick with it before I turn loose this vicious dog of mine. He really wants to go at you now, believe it."

"We won't take advantage of your good nature, Esteban," assured Gomez. "We only came to kill you and rob you of your two burros. Come on down. It's very hot, and we have walked a long way up the river."

"Oh, all right," agreed the old man. "But first call off that demented creature at the base of my tree. You better tie him up some place, too. My man-killing dog may want to go after him. But of course I will do my best to restrain him. Here I come."

"Many thanks, *anciano*," said Gomez. "Give me a moment."

He went up to Perro and told him he could stop barking and jumping at the tree; the matter was settled. But Perro was warmed to his work. He turned on Gomez and showed his teeth. The proprietor of the Golondrina backed away, calling upon Pato for protection. The latter looked about. His eye fell upon Esteban's old ratcatcher dozing on the nearby window sill. Picking up the mangy beast, he stroked her a moment, then dropped her upon the ground immediately in front of the growling Perro. The cat swelled up enormously, spit into the eye of the boy giant who was down on all fours, then ran for the goat shed. Perro churned the earth in the eagerness of his pursuit. But no sooner had he raced into the shed than he was back out of it. Now he was yowling in pain, the old cat hooked securely to his nose. There was one visible refuge for Perro, the watering trough beside the burro corral. Into this the big lad dived. Old pussycat, not caring to drown, released her claws and swam for the trough's edge. All the way back to her sunny window sill she shook each wet paw as she picked it up and before she set it down again. She was dozing once more before Perro slunk out of the trough to hide whimpering beneath its cover.

"Now," announced Esteban Miraflor, sliding out of the acacia tree, "let us go into my humble *casa* and see what this bandit business is all about. I have a little *aguardiente* saved for just such an important occasion. . . . Hmmmm, bandits, you say? Now there's a profession which I have often thought might bring a tidy profit. Yes, yes."

"Aguardiente?" Pato squinted. "You are sure you said *aguardiente*, host?"

"That's what I said." The old man nodded. "Come on."

They started for the door of the adobe.

"Well, all right," accepted Pato. "We won't need to get to the robbing or the killing in such a hurry. Isn't that what you say, jefe?" he inquired of Gomez, who was tagging along absently. "Pleasure before business, eh, my leader?"

Gomez bobbed his bullet head. "Yes, sure," he said, "of course. You heard me. You have your orders, teniente."

"Aguardiente?" repeated Pato, ignoring him to cling to old Miraflor. "The real *aguardiente?* In a hovel like this? Hard to believe, *anciano.* You must mean pulque or perhaps mescal, happily."

"Aguardiente," insisted the old man. "A gift from my nephew who is a priest in Ciudad Obregon."

"A lie," said Pato. "But we will call it whatever you wish. God's name," he said, halting just inside the hut, "it is dark as a bat's cave in here. How do you see?"

"When the vision fades with years," replied Miraflor, "light is the enemy of good seeing. One moment, *hombres*, and you will see well enough.

From a place behind the door, and as his two guests stood in the middle of the dirt floor blinking like barn owls to adjust their eyes to the hut's pitlike darkness, the old man plucked a stout cudgel and struck first Pato and then Gomez expertly and squarely across the backs of their sombreros.

The bandit pair slumped to the floor, senseless.

"Now let me see," said Esteban Miraflor. "Where did I put that jug of *aguardiente?"*

The first matter was to dispose of witnesses. The single one of importance was the bumbling giant boy known as Perro. Esteban glanced outside. Perro was still crouched beneath the watering trough. The old man picked up a stick of kindling and stepped outside. Whistling, he attracted Perro's attention. Seeing the stick, Perro came out from under the trough, his troubles with Madame Gata forgotten on the moment. He bounded toward Esteban and made ready to retrieve the stick.

"Aha," said the old fellow soberly. "A fine dog."

He drew back his arm and threw the stick carefully. It sailed in a high arc, Perro setting off barking in vigorous pursuit. The stick made a graceful parabolic curve and slanted downward to fall with a splash into the deep ranchyard well of Esteban Miraflor. Never pausing, the brave Perro leaped after it. The splash he made was larger and more magnificent in every way, but accompanied by a delayed and howling protest which, to a heart less hard than that of the *hacendado* of the Rio Zorrillo, would have brought immediate humane second thoughts.

"Be patient," advised Esteban Miraflor. "I shall return after a while."

Going inside the house, he carried out the two unconscious bandits and placed them like sacks of shelled corn across the backs of the burros, Bustamante and Chapultepec. Across his own back he slung the jug of *aguardiente*. With a cheery whistle to his ragged mongrel, he was off down the river path, driving the two burros before him.

In due time he came to the old Tehuantltux crossing and the site of the Golondrina.

He drove the burros inside the cantina. There, he took the still slumbering bodies of Gomez and Pato and propped them up at the dark corner table where Perro customarily dwelled. With care and consummate stinginess, he poured a half cup of *aguardiente* upon the head of each sleeper. Into the tilted-back mouth of the unconscious revelers he poured a very small bit of the fiery liquor, just enough to "give them the taste," as he thought of it, as well as the rank odor of the stuff provided by the amount poured over the pates of the two bandits.

Next he put a stub of candle on the corner table and lit it. He lit also the lamp on the bar.

Returning to the table, he held the jug of *aguardiente* up to the light, hefting it. Finding it nearly empty, he drained it of its contents, smacked his lips, and laid the emptied jug upon the table between the slack-mouthed celebrants.

Realizing, from some mutterings and stirrings of his would-be assassins, that they were in some danger of regaining their senses, the old man rolled the four barrels of wine which were the Golondrina's entire commercial supply from behind Gomez's bar and fastened them, slung two and two, on the sturdy backs of Chapultepec and Bustamante. Whistling up his dog, he drove the burros out of the cantina and back up the river bank. Within the hour, he was once more returned to his rancho.

Storing his plunder in the adobe hut, he windlassed the still-yelping Perro up out of the well and advised him that it was growing dark. "If you wish to reach your home before the moon rises," he said, "you had best be about the journey."

Perro uttered a bark of gratitude and broke into a lope on all fours down the river path. When, quite soon, he came up to the open doorway of the Golondrina, still wet from the water of old Miraflor's well, he heard the first arousing profanities of his two friends. Rushing inside at once, he jumped up on them, licking their faces and whining eagerly and completing in this manner the awakening of the would-be outlaws.

When Gomez and Pato had cleared their eyes and their brains from the cobwebs of the cudgel blows of Esteban Miraflor's trick upon them, they still could not recall their true plight.

All they knew was that they must have had one memorable celebration upon someone's *aguardiente*. Who might deny it? There before them on the table was the emptied evidence of their great good time—that and the magnificent headaches they were now having. As for the Golondrina, nothing in it appeared to have changed. It was only when, some moments later, Gomez went behind the bar that he discovered the theft of the four barrels of wine. Outraged, he and Pato ran out into the dusty track which passed in front of the Golondrina. Dashing wildly along the sometime road toward the river and toward where the small city of Tehuantltux stood upon the far side of the stream, they raised their indignant voices in citizen protest.

"Thief, thief! Help, help!" they cried. "Bandits, bandits! We have been robbed!"

Following them out of the dirt-floored cantina, faithful Perro watched after them, cupping his ear and cocking his shaggy head to hear what it was his good friends shouted with such conviction. When he had made out the sense of the words, the huge boy panted and barked and jumped around delightedly in the dust of the roadway to show his loyal agreement.

"A true thing, *compañeros,*" he shouted in his high voice. "Very true."

THE TALLEST INDIAN IN TOLTEPEC

Where the wagon road from the small town of Toltepec, in the state of Chihuahua, came up to the Rio Grande, the fording place was known as the old Apache Crossing. This was because the Indians used it in their shadowy traffic in and out of Texas from Old Mexico. It was not a place of good name, and only those traveled it who, for reasons of their own, did not care to go over the river at the new Upper Crossing.

This fact of border life was well understood by Colonel Fulgencio Ortega. He had not forgotten the Indian back door to El Paso on the American side. That is why he had taken personal charge of the guard post of his troops at this point.

A very crafty man, Colonel Ortega.

And efficient.

It was not for nothing that the *descamisados*, the starving shirtless poor, called him the Executioner of Camargo. Chihuahua had no more distinguished son, nor another son half so well known in the ranks of the irregular *rurales*, which was to say the stinking buzzards of the border.

Now, with his men, a score of brutes so removed from decency and discipline that only their upright postures stamped them as human beings, he lounged about the ashes of the supper fire. Some of the bestial soldiers bickered over the cleaning of the mess kits. Others sat hunched about a serape spread on the ground, belching and complaining of the foulness of their luck with the cards and with the kernels of shelled corn which passed for money among them. The heat of the evening was stifling. Even with the sun now down at last beyond the Rio, it was still difficult to breathe with comfort. The horseflies from the nearby picket line still buzzed and bit like rabid foxes. It was a most unpromising situation. In all of the long daylight they had wasted at the ford, no fish had come to their net, no traveler from Toltepec had sought to pass the crude barricade flung across the wagon road.

"Válgame!" announced Ortega. "God's name, but this is slow work, eh, Chivo?"

The name meant "goat" in Spanish, and the bearded lieutenant who responded to it seemed well described.

"True, jefe." He nodded. "But one learns patience in your service. Also hunger. Hiding. Sand fleas. Body lice. How to use corn for money. How to live on water with no tequila in it. Many things, Excellence."

Ortega smiled and struck him across the face with the butt of his riding quirt. The blow opened the man's face and brought the bright blood spurting.

"Also manners," said the Colonel quietly.

Chivo spat into the dirt. *"Sí,"* he said, "also manners."

Presently, the man on duty at the barricade called to his leader that someone was coming on the road.

"By what manner?" asked Ortega, not moving to rise.

"A burro cart."

"How many do you see?"

"Two. A man and a boy. Hauling firewood, I think."

"*Pah!* Let them go by."

"We do not search the cart, jefe?"

"For what? Firewood?"

"No, jefe, for *him;* these are Indians who come."

Instantly, Ortega was on his feet. He was at the barricade next moment, Chivo and the others crowding behind. All watched in silence the approach of the small burro cart. Had they begun to pant or growl it would have seemed natural, so like a half circle of wolves they appeared.

On the driver's seat of the cart, Díaz grew pale and spoke guardedly to his small son.

"Chamaco," he said, "these are evil men who await us. Something bad may happen. Slip away in the brush if there is any opportunity. These are the enemies of our leader."

"You know them, Papa, these enemies of our Presidente?"

"I know the one with the whip. It is Ortega."

"The Executioner?" The boy whispered the dread name, and Juliano Díaz, slowing the plodding team of burros, answered without moving his head or taking his eyes from the soldiers at the barricade.

"Yes, my son. It is him, the Killer of Camargo. As you value your life, do not speak the name of El Indio except to curse it. These men seek his life."

El Indio was the name of love which the shirtless ones had given the revolutionary President whom they had brought to power with their blood, but who now fought desperately for the life of his new government and for the freedoms which he sought to bring to the *descamisados* of all Mexico, be they Indians, such as himself and Juliano and Chamaco Díaz, or of the Spanish blood, or of any blood whatever. To the small boy, Chamaco, El Indio was like Christ, only more real. He had never seen either one, but he knew he would die for his Presidente and was not so sure about the Savior.

He nodded, now, in response to his father's warning, brave as any ten-year-old boy might be in facing the Executioner of Camargo.

As for Ortega, perhaps the sinister appelation was only a product of ignorance and rebelliousness on the parts of the incredibly poor Indians of the Motherland. He understood this for himself, it was certain. But being a soldier was hard work, and the people never comprehended the necessity for the precautions of military control. This did not mean that one of the Spanish blood could not be gracious and kind within the limitations of his stern duty. The Colonel waved his whip pleasantly enough toward the burro cart.

"Good evening, citizen," he greeted Díaz. "You are surprised to see us here, no doubt. But the delay will be slight. Please to get down from the cart."

"*¿Qué pasa*, Excellence. What is the matter?" In his fear, Díaz did not obey the request to step down but sat numbly on the seat.

"Ah, you know me!" Ortega was pleased. "Well, it has been my work to get acquainted among the people of El Indio. Did you hear my order?"

"What?" said Díaz. "I forget. What did you say, Colonel?"

Ortega moved as a coiled snake might move. He struck out with his whip, its thong wrapping the thin neck of Juliano Díaz. With a violent heave, the guerrilla leader threw the small man from the cart onto the ground, the noose of the whip nearly cracking his vertebrae.

"I said to get down, *Indio*." He smiled. "You do not listen too well. What is the matter? Do you not trust your Mexican brothers?"

Díaz was small in body only. In heart he was a mountain.

"You are no brothers of mine!" he cried. "I am an Indian!"

"Precisely," answered Ortega, helping him up from the dirt of the roadway. "And so is he whom we seek."

Díaz stood proudly, stepping back and away from the kind hands of Colonel Fulgencio Ortega. He made no reply, now, but the boy on the seat of the burro cart leaped down and answered for him.

"What!" he exclaimed, unable to accept the fact anyone would truly seek to do ill to the beloved Presidente. "Is it true then that you would harm our dear—" Too late, he remembered his father's warning and cut off his words. Ortega liked boys, however, and made allowances for their innocence.

"Calm yourself, little rooster," he said kindly. "I said nothing of harming El Indio. Indeed, I said nothing of your great Presidente in any way. Now how is it you would have the idea that it is *him* we look for, eh?"

All of Mexico knew the answer to the question. For weeks the outlands had thrilled to the whisper that El Indio would make a journey to the United States to find gold and the hand of friendship from the other great Presidente, Abraham Lincoln. It was understood such a journey would be in secret to avoid the forces of the enemy en route. But from Oaxaca to the Texas border the *desca-*

misados were alerted to be on the watch for "the Little Indian" and to stand at all times ready to help forward the fortunes of his journey.

Chamaco Díaz hesitated, not knowing what to say.

His father, brave Juliano, broke into the growing stillness to advise him in this direction.

"Say nothing, my son," he said quietly, and stood a little taller as he said it.

Chamaco nodded. He, too, straightened and stood tall beside his father.

They would talk no more, and Ortega understood this.

"My children," he said, "you have failed to comprehend. We do not seek to harm the Presidente, only to detain him."

If standing tall, Chamaco was still but a small boy. He had not learned the art of dishonesty.

"Why do you stop *us*, then, Colonel?" he demanded. "We are only poor wood gatherers from Toltepec, going to El Paso."

"Just exactly my problem," explained Ortega, with a flourish of the whip. "You see, *pobrecito*, it is my order that every Indian going across the border must be measured against that line which you will see drawn on that dead oak tree." He pointed to the sunblasted spar with the whip. "Do you see the line on the tree?"

"Yes, Colonel."

"Well, it is drawn five feet from the ground, *chico*. That is just about the tallness of your great Presidente, not being too precise. Now the problem is that I, myself, am not familiar with this great man. I would not know him if I saw him. But we have his height reported to us, and I have devised this method of—shall we say?—ruling out the chance that El Indio shall get over the river into the United States and complete his journey."

"Colonel," broke in Juliano Díaz, going pale despite his great courage, "what is it you are saying?"

Ortega shrugged good-naturedly.

"Only that if you are an Indian not known to me, or to my men, and if your height is the same as that of El Indio, and if I detain you, then I have prevented a possible escape of your great Presidente, eh?"

"You mean that you think I, Juliano Díaz of Toltepec, am—" He could not finish the thought, so absurd was it to his simple mind. Could this rebel colonel truly believe such a thing? That he, Díaz, was the leader, the great El Indio? Díaz gave his first hint of a relieved look. It may even have been the trace of a smile. There was, after all, and even with the sore neck from the whip, something ironic about the idea. "Please, Excellence," Díaz concluded, forcing the small smile to widen for the sake of Chamaco's courage, "take me to the tree and put me against the mark, that my son and I may go on to El Paso. I have not been well, and we need the pesos from this wood to buy medicine in Texas."

"Chivo," snapped Ortega, no longer smiling, "measure this Indian!"

Chivo seized Díaz and dragged him to the tree. Pushing him against its scarred trunk, he peered at the line.

"He comes exactly to it, jefe. Just the right size."

"Very well. Detain him."

The matter was finished for Colonel Ortega. He turned back to the fire. He did not look around at the pistol shot which blew out the brains of Juliano Díaz. To a scrofulous sergeant, even with the startled, sobbing cry of Chamaco Díaz rising behind him, he merely nodded irritably. "Coffee, Portales. Santa Maria, but it is hot! Curse this river country."

What would have been the fate of Chamaco, the son, no man may say. Chivo was hauling him to the fire by the nape of his neck, pistol poised to finish him as well, with the Colonel's permission. Also, no man may say if Ortega would have granted the favor. For in the instant of death's hovering, a thunder of hooves arose on the American side of the river and a rider, tall sombrero proclaiming his Mexican identity, dashed his lathered mount across the ford and to a sliding stop by the fire of the Executioner of Camargo.

"Colonel!" he cried. "I come from El Paso! Great news is there. El Indio is in the town. He has already been to see the American Presidente and is on his way back to Mexico!"

Ortega stepped back as though cut in the face with his

own whip. The wolf pack of his men drew in upon him. Chivo, in his astonishment that El Indio had gotten out of Mexico and was ready to come back into it, dropped his rough hands from Chamaco Díaz. It was all the signal from above that the quick-witted Indian youth needed. In one scuttling dive he had reached the crowding growth of the river brush and disappeared, faithful, belatedly, to his dead father's instruction.

Chivo, pistol still smoking, led the yelping rush of the guerrilla band after the boy. Ortega cursed on his men, raging about himself with the lashing whip.

"Kill him, you fools!" he screamed. "He must not get over the river. Shoot! Shoot! Stomp him out and shoot him. He must not warn the Americans that we know they have El Indio! After him, after him, you idiots!"

Deep in the brush, Chamaco wriggled and squirmed and raced for his life. The rifle bullets of the renegades cut the limbs about him. The cruel thorns of the mesquite and catclaw and black chaparral ripped his flesh. He could hear the soldiers panting and cursing within a stone's toss of his heels. He cried for his dead father as he ran, but he ran! If God would help him, he would reach the other side of the river and El Indio.

As the desperate vow formed in his mind, he saw ahead a clearing in the tangled growth. Beyond it, the waters of the Rio Grande flowed silver-red in the sunset dusk.

Riding through the twilight toward El Paso, the thoughts of Charlie Shonto were scarcely designed to change the sunburned leather mold of his features—not, at least, for the happier.

A job was a job, he supposed, but it seemed to him that all the while the work got harder and the pay less.

Who the hell was he, Charlie Shonto? And what the devil was the Texas Express Company? And why should the two names cause him pain, now, as he clucked to his weary buckskin and said softly, aloud, "Slope along, little horse, there's good grass and water awaiting."

Well, there was an affinity betwixt the likes of Charlie Shonto and the Texas Express Company, even if it hurt. The latter outfit was a jerkwater stage line that had gotten itself about as rump-sprung as a general freight and passenger operation might manage to do and still harness four sound horses, and Shonto was a "special agent" for the stage company. But Charlie Shonto did not let the fancy title fool him. There was a shorter term, and a deal more accurate, for the kind of work he did for Texas Express. If a man said it with the proper curl of lip, it came out something awfully close to "hired gun."

Shonto didn't care for the label. He didn't especially relish, either, the risks involved in wearing it. But a "riding gun," be he on the driver's box with an L. C. Smith or Parker on his lap, or in the saddle with a Winchester booted under his knee, made good money for the better jobs. The better jobs, of course, were those in which the survival odds were backed down to something like, or less than, even money. So it was no surprise to Shonto to be sent for by Texas Express for a "special assignment." The surprise might lie in the assignment, itself, but the sun-tanned rider doubted it. It could be assumed that when Texas Express sent for Charlie Shonto, the "opportunity for advancement" was one already turned down by the Rangers and the U.S. Army, not to mention Wells Fargo, Overland Mail, or any of the big staging outfits.

Shonto clucked again to the *bayo coyote*, the line-backed buckskin dun, that he rode.

"Just around the bend, Butterball." He grinned dustily. "Billet for you and bullets for me."

Butterball, a gaunt panther of a horse which appeared wicked and rank enough to eat rocks without spitting out the seeds, rolled an evil eye back at his master and flagged the ragged pennant of his left ear. If he had intended further comment than this one look of tough disgust, the urge was short-circuited.

Scarcely had the comment about "bullets" left Shonto's lips than a respectable, if well-spent, hail of them began to fall around him in the thicket. Next instant, the sounds of the rifle shots were following the leaden advance guard in scattered volleys.

Instinctively, he ticked Butterball with the spurs, and the bony gelding sprinted like a quarter-mile racer for the near bend ahead. When he brought Shonto around that bend, the latter hauled him up sharply. Across the Rio Grande a tattered company of Mexican irregulars were target-practicing at a dark, bobbing object in midstream. Shonto's immediate reaction was one of relief that the riflemen had not been firing at him. The next thought was a natural curiosity as to what they had been firing at. It was then the third message reached his tired mind, and his mouth went hard. *That was a little kid swimming for the American side out there.*

The night was well down. In the Texas Express office in El Paso, three men waited. The drawn shade, trimmed lamp, the tense glances at the wall clock ticking beyond the way-bill desk, all spoke louder than the silence.

"I wish Shonto would get here," complained the express agent, Deems. "It ain't like him to be late. Maybe Ortega crossed over the river under dark and blind-sided him."

The second man, heavy-set, dressed in eastern clothing, calm and a little cold, shook his head.

"Shonto isn't the type to be blind-sided, Deems. You forget he's worked for me before. I didn't exactly pull his name out of a hat."

Deems stiffened. "That don't mean Ortega didn't pull it out of a sombrero!"

Sheriff Nocero Casey, last of the trio, nodded.

"Deems is right, Mr. Halloran. I don't care for Charlie being late either. It *ain't* like him. If Ortega did hear we had sent for Charlie Shonto—" He broke off, scowling.

Halloran took him up quickly. "It's not Shonto being late that is really bothering you, is it? I counted on you, Sheriff. I didn't dare import a bunch of U.S. marshals. I hope you're not getting cold feet."

"No, sir. It's common sense I'm suffering from. This job is way out of my bailiwick. The government ought to send troops or something to see it through. It's too big."

Again Halloran shook his head. "The U.S. government can't set one toe across that river, Sheriff. You know that. It's the law. That's why we've brought in your 'special agent.' Mr. Shonto is a man who understands the law. He appreciates its niceties, its challenges."

"Yeah, I've often wondered about that," said the Sheriff. "But I won't argue it."

"Ah, good. You see, there is no law which says Texas Express cannot ship a consignment such as our invaluable Item Thirteen into Toltepec. It will be done every day now that the new Mexican Central line has reached that city."

Agent Deems interrupted this optimism with a groan.

"Good Lord, Mr. Halloran, what's the use of talking about what we can ship when that cussed Mexican Central Railroad starts running regular between Toltepec and Mexico City? They ain't even run one work engine over that new line that I know of. Them blamed ties that are laid into Toltepec are still oozing greenwood sap!"

Halloran's heavy jaw took a defiant set.

"Are your feet feeling the chill, also, Deems? I thought we had the plan agreed to. Where's the hitch?"

Agent Deems stared at his questioner as if the latter had taken leave of whatever few senses government secret service operatives were granted in the beginning.

"Where's the hitch, you say? Oh, hardly anywhere at all, Mr. Halloran. You're only asking us to deliver this precious Item Thirteen of yours to railhead in Toltepec, Mexico, fifty miles across the river, tonight, with no one wise, whatever, right square through Colonel Fulgencio Ortega's northern half of the loyalist guerrilla army, guaranteeing to get our 'shipment' on the train at Toltepec safe and sound in wind and limb and then to come back a-grinning and a-shrugging and a-saying, 'Why, shucks, it wasn't nothing. It's done every day.' Mister, you ain't just plain crazy, you're extra fancy nuts."

"As bad as all that, eh?"

"Fair near," put in Sheriff Casey. "We don't know if that Mexican train will be in Toltepec. We don't even know if those wild-eyed coffee beans even *got* a train. All we know is that you government men tell us they got the train, and that it'll be in Toltepec if we get this Item Thirteen there. Now that's a heck of an 'if.' "

Halloran was careful. He knew that only these local people—Texans familiar with every coyote track and kit-fox trail leading into Chihuahua—could bring off the delivery of Item 13. Nothing must go wrong now.

"If we took Item Thirteen five thousand miles, Sheriff, surely Texas Express ought to be able to forward shipment the remaining fifty miles to Toltepec."

"Huh!" said Deems Harter. "You got one whack of a lot more faith in Texas Express than we have. In fact, about forty-nine miles more. As agent, I'll guarantee to get your precious shipment exactly one mile. That's from here to the Rio Grande. Past that, I wouldn't give you a nickel for your chances of making that train in Toltepec. *If* there's a train in Toltepec."

Halloran shook his head, unmoved.

"I'm not exactly thinking of my faith in terms of Texas Express, Harter. It's Charlie Shonto we're all gambling on."

"Yeah," said Harter acridly. "And right now Charlie Shonto looks like a mighty poor gamble."

"Well, anyways," broke in Sheriff Nocero Casey, who had drifted to the front window for another look up the street, "a mighty wet one. Yonder comes our special delivery man, and it looks to me as though he's already been across the river. He's still dripping."

Halloran and Harter joined him in peering from behind the drawn shade. It was the express agent who recovered first.

"Good Lord!" he gasped. "What's that he's toting behind him?"

Sheriff Nocero Casey squinted carefully.

"Well," he said, "the bright lights of El Paso ain't precisely the best to make bets by, but if I had to take a scattergun guess at this distance and in the dark, I'd say it was a sopping-wet and some-undersized Chihuahua Indian boy."

In the shaded office of the Texas Express Company, the silence had returned again. First greetings were over. Shonto and Halloran had briefly touched upon their past experiences during the war between the states, and the time had very quickly run down to that place where everyone pauses, knowing that the next words are the ones that the money is being paid for. Sheriff Casey, Agent Harter, Shonto, even little Chamaco Díaz, all were watching P. J. Halloran.

"Now, Charlie," said the latter, at last, "we haven't sent for you to review the squeaks you've been in before." He let the small grimace which may or may not have been a smile pass over his rough features. "But I did feel that some slight mention of our past associations might prepare you for the present proposal."

"What you're saying, Mr. Halloran, is that you figure your Irish blarney is going to soften up my good sense."

Shonto's own grin was a bit difficult to classify. It was hard as flint and yet warmed too, somehow, by a good nature or at least a wry appreciation of life as it actually worked out in the living.

"But you're wasting your talents," he concluded. "I've had a couple of birthdays since I was crossing the Confederate lines for you, and now I don't sign up just for a pat on the back from my fellow countrymen. I've learned since the war that a man can't buy a bag of Bull Durham with a government citation. Not that I regret my time in the 'silent service,' mind you. But a fellow just doesn't like to be a hog about the hero business. Especially when he did his great deeds for the North, then went back to earning his keep in the South. If you spend your time in Texas, Mr. Halloran, you don't strain yourself reminding the local folks that you took your war pay in Union greenbacks."

Halloran nodded quickly.

"Don't be a fool, Charlie," he said. "Harter, here, and Sheriff Casey were carefully sounded out before we ever mentioned your name. They are not still afire with the Lost Cause. We can forget your war work."

"I'm glad you told me, Mr. Halloran. Somehow, I still remember it every so often. Matter of fact, I still occasionally wake up in a cold sweat. Now I can put all that behind me. Isn't it wonderful?"

"Shonto"—Halloran's hard face had turned cold again—"come over here to the window. I want to show you something." He took a pair of binoculars from Harter's desk, and Shonto followed him to the drawn shade. There,

Halloran gave the glasses to him and said quietly, "Look yonder on the balcony of the Franklin House. Tell me what you see. Describe it exactly."

From the other's tone, Shonto knew the talk had gotten to the money point. He took the glasses and focused them on the hotel's second-story *galería*, the railed porch so common to the southwestern architecture of the times. As the view came into sharp detail, he frowned uneasily. "All right," he began, low voiced. "I see a man. He's short, maybe not much over five feet. He stands straight as a yardstick. Stocky build. Big in the chest. Dark as hell in the skin, near as I can say in the lamplight from the room windows behind him. He's dressed in a black Eastern suit that don't fit him, and same goes for a white iron collar and necktie. Black hat, no creases, wore square like a sombrero. Long black hair, bobbed off like it was done with horse shears." He paused, squinting more narrowly through the binoculars. "Why," he added softly, "that's a blasted Indian dressed up in white man's clothes!"

"That," said P. J. Halloran, just as softly, "is exactly what it is." They turned from the window. "Up there on that balcony," Halloran continued, "is the most important man, next to Lincoln, in North America. I can't reveal his identity, and you will have to know him as Item Thirteen, until you have him safely on that waiting train at Toltepec."

"What train at Toltepec?" Shonto frowned. "Since when have they built the Mexican Central on into that two-burro burg?"

"Since today, we hope," said Halloran. "The idea was that, precisely as you, no one knew the railroad had been laid on into Toltepec. Those last few thousand yards of track were to be spiked down today. The gamble is that not even Ortega and the *rurales* would hear about it in time. Or, hearing of it, not realize a train was waiting to be run over it."

"That's what I'd call house odds, Mr. Halloran. This Item Thirteen must be one heck of a table-stakes man."

"He's one heck of a man," answered the government operative. "Anyway, Charlie, that train is supposed to be waiting at midnight in Toltepec. If we can get Item Thirteen there, the train can get on down past Camargo by daybreak and out of Ortega's reach—*if* the train's waiting in Toltepec."

"Longest two-letter word in the world," said Shonto. "Go ahead, drop the other boot."

"Well, we know that powerful enemies lie between El Paso and Toltepec. There's no point explaining to you the type of enemy I mean. I believe you're familiar enough with Colonel Ortega and his loyal militia."

"Yes, just about familiar enough. In case you're still wondering how Chamaco and I got ourselves doused in the Rio, it was meeting Ortega's loyal army, or as big a part of it as I came prepared to handle. I'd say there was twenty of them. They were pot-shooting at the kid swimming the river. He got away from them while they were murdering his father. Butterball got excited at the rifle fire and ran away with me: bolted right into the river. Next thing I knew, I was in as bad shape as the kid, and, long as I figured two could ride as cheap as one, I scooped him up and we made it back to the American side by way of hanging onto Butterball's tail and holding long breaths under water on the way. I have got to get me another horse. In my business, you can't be fooling around with jumpy crowbaits like that."

"When you decide what you want for Butterball," put in Sheriff Nocero Casey, "let me know. I've been looking for just such a loco horse."

"Charlie," broke in Halloran, "are you interested or not? We've got to move soon."

Shonto nodded speculatively, a man not to be rushed. "Depends. You haven't dropped that other boot yet."

"All right." Halloran spoke quickly now. "The small man in the black suit carries a letter of credit—a U.S. letter of credit—for an enormous amount of money. Some say as high as fifty million dollars. That's fifty million U.S., not Mexican. It's to bail out his revolution down there." Halloran gestured toward the Rio Grande and Mexico. "I don't need to tell you, Charlie, what men like Ortega will do to prevent that letter from getting to Mexico City. The money means the rebels are through—loyalists, they call themselves—and that the revolution will succeed and will stay in power. As you have already learned when your horse ran away with you, Colonel Ortega has been assigned the job of sealing off the border in Chihuahua State. Now, it becomes your job to unseal that border."

Charlie Shonto's grin was dry as dust.

"Shucks, nothing to that—nothing that I couldn't do with ten or twelve companies of Rangers and a regiment of regular Cavalry."

"Don't joke, Charlie." Halloran pulled out an official document and handed it to Shonto. "Here are my orders. You don't need to read them. But check that final postscript at the bottom of the page against the signature beneath the Great Seal of this country you and I fought for, when *he* asked us to."

Shonto glanced down the page, reading aloud slowly. " 'Any man who may aid the bearer of these orders in the business to hand will know that the gratitude of his government and my own personal indebtedncss shall be his and shall not be forgotten. [Signed] A. Lincoln.'

"Well now," he said, handing back the document as gingerly as though it were the original of the Declaration of Independence. "Why didn't you say so, Mr. Halloran?"

"Like you"—Halloran smiled, and this time there was no doubt it was a smile—"I always save my best shot for the last target. What do you say, Charlie?"

"I say, let's go. For *him* I'd wrestle a bear, blindfolded. Who all's in it?"

"Just you, Charlie. I've brought our man this far. Sheriff Casey and Agent Harter have handled him here in town. But from here to Toltepec, he's your cargo—*if* you'll accept him."

Shonto winced perceptibly.

"There's that word again. You got anything extra to go with it this time?"

Halloran picked up a rolled map from Harter's desk.

"Only this chart of the area between here and Toltepec supplied by the Mexican Government. You know this ground as well as any man on this side of the Rio Grande. Take a look at this layout of it and tell us if you spot any way at all of getting past Ortega's patrols, into Toltepec."

He spread the map on the desk. Harter turned up the wick, and the four men bent over the wrinkled parchment. Behind them, the little Indian, Chamaco Díaz, had been forgotten. He stood silently in the shadows, wondering at the talk of these *Americans*. Chamaco had been to school some small time in El Paso and knew enough English to follow the conversation in the rough. Lonely and sorrowful as he was, he knew who that other little Indian in the black suit was, and his heart swelled with love and pride for these *American* men, that they would talk of risking their lives that El Indio might live and might reach *Mexico City* with the United States money which would save the Presidente's brave government of the *descamisados* and *pobrecitos* such as his father, Juliano Díaz, who had given their lives to establish it. Now, Chamaco watched the four big *Americans* bent over the map of Toltepec—his part of the beloved Motherland—and he waited with held breath what the verdict of the one tall man with the dried leather face would be.

For his part, the latter was having considerable last doubts. The map wasn't showing him anything he didn't already know. Presently, he glanced up at Halloran.

"There's no help here," he said. "I was hoping to see an old Apache route I've heard stories of. But this map shows nothing that wouldn't get me and the little man in the black suit stood up against the same tree that Chamaco's daddy was stood up against. Ortega knows all these trails."

"There's nothing, then? No way at all?"

"Yes, there's that Apache brush track. It was never found by the Rangers, but they know it exists. They've run the Chihuahua Apaches right to the river, time and again, then seen them vanish like smoke into midnight air. If we knew where that trail went over the Rio, we might have a coyote's chance of sneaking past Ortega's assassins." Shonto shook his head. "But there isn't a white man alive who knows that Apache track. . . ."

His words trailed off helplessly, and the four men straightened with that weary stiffness which foretells defeat. But into their glum silence a small voice, and forgotten, penetrated thinly.

"Señores, I am not a white man."

Shonto and his companions wheeled about. Chamaco moved out of the shadows into the lamplight.

"I am an Indian," he said, "and I know where the old trail runs."

The four men exchanged startled looks and, in their momentary inability to speak, Chamaco thought that he detected reproof for his temerity in coming forward in the company of such powerful friends of Mexico. He bowed with apologetic humility and stepped back into the shadows.

"But of course," he said, small-voiced, "you would not trust to follow an Indian. Excuse me, *Señores."*

Shonto moved to his side. He put his hand to the thin shoulder. Telling the boy to follow him, he led the way to the office window. He held back the drawn shade while Chamaco, obeying him, peered down the street at the Franklin House.

"Boy," he said, "do you know who that small man is standing up there on the hotel balcony?"

Chamaco's eyes glowed with the fire of his pride.

"Yes, patrón!" he cried excitedly. "It is *him!* Who else could stand and look so sad and grand across the river?"

Shonto nodded. "You think *he* would trust an Indian boy?"

Chamaco drew himself up to his full four feet and perhaps five inches. In his reply was all the dignity of the poor.

"Patrón," he said, "he once *was* an Indian boy!"

Charlie Shonto nodded again. He tightened the arm about the boy's shoulders and turned to face the others.

"Don't know about you," he said to them, "but I've just hired me an Indian guide to Toltepec."

The men at the desk said nothing, and again Chamaco misinterpreted their hesitation.

"Patrón," he said to Charlie Shonto, "do *you* know who it is up there standing on the *galería* looking so sad toward Mexico?"

"I could take an uneducated guess," answered Shonto, "but I won't. You see, Chamaco, I'm not supposed to know. He's just a job to me. It doesn't matter who he is."

The Indian boy was astounded. It passed his limited comprehensions.

"And you would risk your life for a stranger to you?" he asked, unbelievingly. "For an Indian in a rumpled white man's suit? A small funny-looking man with a foreign hat and long hair and a dark skin the same as mine? You would do this, patrón, and for nothing?"

Shonto grinned and patted him on the head.

"Well, hardly for nothing, boy."

"For what, then, patrón?"

"Money, boy. Pesos. Muchos pesos."

"And only for that, patrón?"

At the persistence, Shonto's cynical grin faded. He made a small, deprecatory gesture. It was for Chamaco alone; he had forgotten the others.

"Let's just say that I was watching your face when you looked up at that hotel balcony a minute ago. All right, *amigo?"*

The dark eyes of Chamaco Díaz lit up like altar candles.

"Patrón," he said, "you should have been an Indian; you have eyes in your heart!"

Shonto grinned ruefully. "Something tells me, boy, that before we get our cargo past Ortega tonight we'll be wishing I had those eyes in the back of my head."

Chamaco reached up and took the gunman's big hand. He patted it reassuringly. "Patrón"—he smiled back—"do not be afraid. If we die, we die in a good and just cause. We lose only our two small lives. Him, up there on the *galería,* he has in his hands the lives of all the poor people of Mexico. Is that not a very fair exchange, our lives for all of those others, and for his?"

Shonto glanced at the other men. "Well, Chamaco," he said, "that's one way of looking at it. Excuse us, gentlemen; we've got a train to catch in Toltepec."

He took the boy's hand in his and they went out into the street. Halloran moved to follow them. At the door he halted a moment, shaking his head as he looked back at the express agent and the sheriff.

"Do you know what we've just done?" he said. "We've just bet fifty million dollars and the future of Mexico on a Chihuahua Indian kid not one of us ever laid eyes on prior to twenty minutes ago. I need a drink!"

The coach bounced and swayed through the night. Its side lamps, almost never lit, were now sputtering and smoking. They seemed to declare that this particular old Concord wanted to be certain her passage toward the lower ford would be noted from the far side—and followed.

The idea was valid.

The lower crossing, the old Apache route, was the way in which a mind of no great deception might seek to elude examination by the *rurales* at the upper, or main, crossing. The driver of the old Texas Express vehicle, a canvas topped Celerity model made for desert speed, held the unalterable belief that the Mexican mind was so devious as to be very nearly simple. It twisted around so many times in its tracks, trying to be clever, that in the end it usually wound up coming right back where it started.

The driver was banking on this trait. He was depending on Colonel Fulgencio Ortega to think that, when the planted rumor from El Paso reached him by avenue of his kinsmen in that city, he would say, "Aha! This stupid *American* stage-line company thinks that if they announce they will try to cross with El Indio at the old lower ford, that I shall at once conclude they really mean to cross at the new upper ford, and that I shall then be waiting for them at the new upper ford and they can cross in safety at the lower place. What fools! I shall quite naturally watch both crossings, and this they realize full well. What they are trying to do is see that I, personally, am not at the lower ford. They think that if they can contest the crossing with my men—without me—it will be a far easier matter. Well, now! ¡*Ai, Chihuahua!* Let them come. Let them find out who will be waiting for their disreputable stagecoach and its mysterious passenger at the old lower ford! Hah! Why will they attempt to match wits with the Executioner of Camargo?"

Of course, if Colonel Ortega did not reason thus, the driver of the coach would have made a grievous error, for the entire plan depended on meeting the Executioner.

The driver, a weatherbeaten, leathery fellow, wrapped the lines of the four-horse hitch a bit tighter. He spoke to his leaders and his wheelers, tickling the ears of the former and the haunches of the latter with the tip of his fifteen-foot coaching whip.

"Coo-ee, boys!" he called to the horses. "Just so, just so." Leaning over the box, he spoke to the muffled, dark-faced passenger—the only passenger—in the rocking stage. *"Señor,* it is all well with you in there?" He used the Spanish tongue, but no reply came in kind from the interior. Indeed, no reply came in any tongue.

A very brave fellow, thought the driver. His kind were not many in the land below the Rio—or any land.

"You are a very small boy," said the somber-looking little man. "How is it that you are so brave?"

"Please, Presidente. I beg of you not to say more, just now. We are very near to the place, and there is great danger." Chamaco spoke with awed diffidence.

"I am not afraid, boy." El Indio patted him on the shoulder. "Do I not have a good Indian guide?"

"Presidente, please, say no more. You don't know Colonel Ortega."

"I have dealt with his kind. I know him, all right. They are all alike. Cowards. Jackals. Don't be afraid, boy. What did you say your name was?"

Chamaco told him, and the small man nodded.

"A good Indian name. It means what it says. How much farther now, boy, before we cross the river?"

They were moving through a tunneled avenue in the river's brushy scrub of willow and rushes. It was the sort of thoroughfare frequented by the creatures of the night. None but very small men—or boys—might have used it at all, and then only very small Indian men or boys. If the Rangers had wanted to know one reason, just one, why the Apaches raiding up from Chihuahua had been able to disappear before their eyes on the American side of the Rio, it would have been that they were seeking some "hole" in the brush which would accommodate an ordinary mortal, not a Chihuahua Indian. But Chamaco Díaz was not alone a small Indian boy; he was a patriot.

"Presidente," he now pleaded, "will you not be quiet? *Por favor*, Excellence! We are coming to it this moment."

The small man in the black suit smiled.

"You dare to address me in this abrupt manner!" he said. "You, an Indian boy? A shirtless waif of the border? A brush rat of the river bottom? *Ai!*"

"Presidente," said the boy, "I will ask it one more time. I know that you do not fear the Executioner. I know that I am only a *pobrecito,* a *reducido,* a nothing. But in my heart you live with the Lord Jesus. I will die for you, Presidente, as I would for Him, even sooner. But I have sworn to guide you across the river and to the rendezvous. I have sworn to get you to Toltepec by midnight this night. Therefore, why should we die, when you must live for the people of our suffering land? I am taking you to Toltepec, Presidente. And if you continue to speak along the way, I will die for nothing and Mexico will never get the money you bear and she will not be saved. But mostly, Presidente, you will be dead. I cannot bear that. You are the life of all of us."

They had stopped moving. El Indio, in a streak of moonlight penetrating the arched limbs above them, could see the tears coursing down the dark cheeks of Chamaco Díaz. He reached quickly with his fingers and brushed away the tears.

"An Indian does not weep," he told the boy sternly. "Go ahead, now. I shall be still."

Chamaco swallowed hard. He dashed his own hand quickly at the offending eyes. His voice was vibrant with pride.

"It was the brush, Presidente, the small limbs snapping back and stinging me across the face. You know how it is."

El Indio nodded once more.

"Of course, boy. I have been in the brush many times.

Go ahead, show the way. I have been an old woman, talking too much. We are both Indians, eh? Lead on."

Straight as a rifle barrel, Chamaco Díaz stood before him a moment. Then, ducking down again, he scuttled on ahead. El Indio watched him go. Just before he bent to follow, he glanced up at the patch of moonlight. The beams struck his own dark face. They glistened on something which seemed to be moist and moving upon his own coffee-colored features. But then of course in moonlight the illusions are many, and the lunar eye is not to be trusted. Had he not just said, himself, that Indians did not weep?

The coach of the Texas Express Company splashed over the old Apache Crossing and came to a halt before the flaring bonfire and wooden barricade across the Toltepec road. "*¿Qué pasa?*" the tall driver called down to the leering brigand who commanded the guard. "What is the matter? Why do you stop me?"

"*De nada.* It is nothing." Lieutenant Chivo smiled. "A small matter which will take but a moment. I hope you have a moment. *"Yes? Very well. Colonel,"* he called to the squat officer drinking coffee by the fireside, "the stage for Toltepec has arrived on time."

The Colonel put down his tin cup and picked up a long quirt. Uncoiling the whip, he arose and came over to the barricade. He stood a moment looking up at the coachman. After a moment, he nodded pleasantly enough and spoke in a friendly manner.

"Please to get down," he said.

"Sorry, I can't do it," replied the driver. "Company rules, Colonel. You understand."

"Of course," said the guerrilla chief easily. "Without rules nothing is accomplished. I'm a great believer in discipline. Did I introduce myself? Colonel Fulgencio Ortega, of Camargo. Now do you care to get down?"

"*The* Colonel Ortega?" said the American driver, impressed. "Jefe, this a great honor. And these are your famed *rurales?*" He pointed with unqualified admiration to the surly pack stalking up, now, to stand behind the colonel and his lieutenant. "My, but they are a fine-looking troop. Real fighters, one can see that. But then, why not? On the side of justice all men fight well, eh, Colonel?"

Ortega ignored the compliments.

"Did you hear what I said?" he asked. "I wish you to get down. I do not believe I have met your passenger, and I think you should introduce me to him. My men will hold your horses."

His men were already holding the horses, as the driver was keenly aware. Also, he did not miss the fact the soldiers were holding something else for him: their rifles—pointed squarely at him. But he was the steady sort, or perhaps merely stupid.

"Passenger?" he said. "I carry no passenger, Colonel. Just some freight for Toltepec."

Ortega stepped back. He looked again into the coach.

"Freight, eh?" he mused. "Strange wrappings you have put around your cargo, *cochero*. A black suit. Black hat with round Indian crown worn squarely on the head. And see how your freight sits on the seat of the coach, just as if it were alive and had two arms and two legs and might speak if spoken to. That is, if fear has not sealed its cowardly Indian tongue!" His voice was suddenly wicked with hatred, all the smile and the pretense of easiness gone out of it—and out of him. "Chivo!" he snapped. "Please to open the door of this coach and help El Presidente to dismount!"

The stage driver straightened on the box.

"El Presidente?" he said to Ortega. "Whatever in the world are you talking about, jefe?"

"We shall see in a moment." Ortega nodded, in control of himself once more. "Hurry, Chivo. This *cochero* does not understand the importance of his passenger. Nor is it apparent to him that jokes about 'freight' which walks and talks like an Indian are not laughed at in Chihuahua just now. *¡Adelante!* Get that coach door opened, you fool!"

Chivo, grinning as only a dog wolf about to soil the signpost of his rival may grin, threw open the door of the Concord and seized the lone passenger by the arm. With a foul-mouthed oath, he pulled the small figure from the coach and hurled it viciously to the ground.

His surprise was understandable.

It is not the usual thing for a victim's arm to come off at the shoulder and remain in the offending hand of its assaulter while the remainder of the torso went flying off through the night. Neither was it the usual thing for the poor devil's head to snap off and go rolling away like a melon when the body thudded to earth.

"*¡Santísima!*" cried one of the brute soldiers of the guard. "You have ruined him, you dumb animal!"

But Lieutenant Chivo did not hear the remark, and Colonel Ortega, if he heard it, did not agree with the sentiment, except perhaps as to Chivo's intelligence. For what the guerrilla lieutenant had pulled from the Texas Express Company's Toltepec stage was quite clearly a dressmaker's dummy, clothed to resemble a very short and large-chested Mexican Indian man who always sat straight on his seat and wore his black hat squarely on his head.

Moreover, Colonel Fulgencio Ortega was given no real time in which to comment upon his soldier's awed remark or his lieutenant's amazed reaction to the arm in his hand and the head rolling free upon the firelit banks of the Rio Grande. For in the small moment of stricken dumbness which had invaded all of the *rurales* when El Presidente's body had come apart in mid-air, the American driver of the Toltepec stage had wrapped the lines of his four-horse hitch, stepped to the ground in one giant stride from the precarious box of the old Concord, and all in the same motion slid out a long-barreled Colt's revolver and buried its iron snout in the belly of the Executioner of Camargo.

"Jefe," he announced quietly. "if you make one false movement, your bowels will be blown out all over this riverbank," and this statement Colonel Fulgencio Ortega had no difficulty whatever in comprehending.

"Chivo!" he cried out. "In the name of María, hold the men. Let no one touch trigger!"

"Yes, Chivo." The leather-faced American *"cochero"* nodded, spinning Ortega around so that the muzzle of the Colt was in his spine. "And so that you do not in greed seek to replace your beloved jefe in command of the *rurales* of Camargo—that is to say, that you do not in this moment of seeming opportunity make some move deliberately to get me to shoot him—permit me to introduce myself."

"Ah?" queried Chivo, who truly had not yet thought of this obvious course of treachery to his leader. "And to what point would this be, *cochero?* Do you think that I am in fear of stagecoach drivers?"

The tall driver shrugged.

"Well, I think you ought to have the same break I give any other man I'm paid to get past."

There was something in the way that he spoke the one word "paid" which penetrated Chivo's wily mind. He hesitated, but two of the soldiers did not. Thinking that they stood well enough behind their companions to be safe, they moved a little aside from the pack to get a line of fire at the big *American.* The instant they were clear of their friends, however, flame burst from behind the back of Colonel Ortega—one lancing flash, then another—and the two soldiers were down and dying in the same blending roar of pistol shots.

"Shonto," said the stage driver to Chivo, the smoking muzzle of the Colt again in Ortega's spine. "Over there across the river, they call me Shonto."

"*¡Madre María!*" breathed Chivo, dropping his rifle, unbidden, into the dirt of the wagon road. "Carlos Shonto? *Por Dios, pistolero*, why didn't you say so?"

"I just did." Charlie Shonto nodded. "Now you better say something. Quick."

Chivo shrugged in that all-meaning way of his kind.

"What remains to die for?" he inquired. "You do not have El Indio in the stage. You have fooled us with the dummy on the ground over there. Somewhere, El Presidente is no doubt riding through the night. But it is not upon the stage for Toltepec. Another of our guards will get him. For us, the work of the day is over. Command me."

Shonto then ordered all the soldiers to drop their rifles and cartridge bandoleers. All knives, pistols, axes went into the common pile. This arsenal was then loaded into the stage along with Colonel Fulgencio Ortega, bound hand and foot by his faithful followers. The work went forward under Chivo's expert direction, the spirit of the *rurales* now totally flagged. With their chances of snaring El Indio had gone their interest in being heroes. Like soldiers everywhere, they were of no great menace in themselves. Deprived of leadership, they were just so many surly dogs quarreling among themselves. Shonto had gambled on this, and gambled exceeding well.

Yet, as in every risk, there lurks the element of the unknown, the thing that cannot be depended upon except in the name of "luck."

Shonto's luck ran out with the command he now issued to the scar-faced Chivo.

"All right, Lieutenant," he said. "Up you go. You'll be the *cochero* now. I'll ride shotgun. You savvy *'la escopeta?'* " With the question, he reached for the double-barreled Parker laid across the driver's box, and Chivo nodded hastily. He "savvied" shotguns very well. One did not argue with them at close range, not ever. But Shonto had made his basic mistake some time ago, when he had put the thought of succeeding to Ortega's place of power in Camargo in the mind of the brutal lieutenant. Such towering aspirations had never flooded his dark brain. True, he would have seen Ortega killed in a moment, should that suit his purpose. This much was exactly what Shonto had guessed. What the wary gunman had not foreseen, however, was that, until he, Shonto, had mentioned the matter, Chivo had never really thought about the possibility of promoting himself over his Colonel.

Now the prospect inflamed his jackal's mind.

"Whatever you say, jefe," he told Shonto, fanging a smirk which the latter hardly supposed was a grin of good nature. "You see, I climb to the seat gladly. I take the lines and am ready to drive for you. Come on. Let's go."

Shonto started to swing up after him. For one moment both hands were occupied. It was in that moment that the boot of Lieutenant Chivo drove into his face. Shonto fell backward, landing hard. The shotgun was still in his grasp but was useless from that angle. Above him, Chivo was shouting the horses into motion. The coach lurched forward. Shonto made it to his feet in time to leap for the trunk straps in the rear. He caught one of them, held on, and dragged behind the moving stage for fifty feet. He still had the shotgun in his right hand.

The soldiers, sensing his helplessness, ran toward him. They seized clubs and picked up rocks on the run. Chivo, in response to their yells, slowed the stage, thinking to allow them to beat and stone the dragging American.

Shonto held onto the trunk strap. When the snarling soldiers were near, he raised the shotgun and fired it with one hand into their faces. The first barrel and the second blasted as one. The soldiers fell away, three to stagger and fall mortally wounded, two others clutching at their shredded faces, screaming in the agony of the immediate torture and the knowledge, even in their terrible pain, that they would never use their eyes again.

Chivo, on the driver's box, turned in time to see Shonto haul himself up over the rear of the Concord. He had no weapon, now, but neither did the *rurale* lieutenant.

Chivo knew the one way open to him and took it. Over the side he went, rolling to the ground and free of the speeding wheels, the excited team running wild the moment he flung away the lines. Shonto, weaving precariously, made it to the driver's box and threw himself down between the straining horses to recover the lines.

His luck now returned. He was able to gather up the lines and return to the box, the coach under control and still upright on the wagon road to Toltepec.

But now he knew the wolf pack behind him had a leader again. He could guess how long it would take Chivo to mount the survivors and take up the pursuit.

"Coo-ee, coo-ee," he called to the snorting team. "Steady down, you beauties. You've not begun your night's work yet. Save that pep and vim for the last lap!"

Where he had said he would be waiting beside the wagon road to Toltepec with El Presidente, there Chamaco Díaz waited when, half an hour's loping run from the Rio, Shonto pulled up his panting horses and hailed the underbrush. The Indian boy had guided his charge without fail and on foot through the night and between the prowling soldiers of Colonel Ortega four miles south of the river. The ancient and secret Apache escape route from Texas, which the two had traveled to reach their rendezvous with Charlie Shonto and the stage for Toltepec, lay still unknown behind them. Shonto did not ask Chamaco where it ran, and the boy did not tell him. He was an Indian, even now, and Charlie Shonto was a white man.

Swiftly, then, the last part of the plan was put into operation. The four horses were unhooked from the coach. Four saddles and bridles were brought from the coach trunk, and the mounts were readied. Colonel Ortega was removed from the stage and hung over the saddle of one mount in the manner of a sack of grain. Shonto tied his hands to his feet under the horse's belly, halfway hoping the ropes would not hold. Where the rutted track of the road bent to go past the rendezvous, an eighty-foot bluff rose above the Chihuahuan plain. Over this drop, Shonto and his two Indian friends now tossed the Concord's load of firearms. There was no time for more effective disposal. Mounting up, the party set out, away from the road, Chamaco leading, Shonto bringing up the rear with the pack horse of the Executioner of Camargo. The goat path along which the small Indian boy took them disappeared into the desert brush within a pistol shot from the wagon road. Shonto had no more idea where the trail led than did Ortego or El Presidente. No options remained in any event. Behind them, along the road from the river, they heard now the shouts of men of Mexican tongue and the hammer of horses' hooves in considerable number. In a pause to listen, they all recognized the high yelping tones of Lieutenant Chivo, discovering the abandoned stage and guessing, amid a goat's beard of rotten curses, the manner of flight of his enemies. And more: from Chivo's murderous bleats, they made out that he had with him another patrol of Ortega's *rurales*, evidently encountered along the way. These new soldiers, whatever their number, would be armed and were clearly being commanded by the Colonel's good lieutenant. All might still have been well

—yes, surely would have been so—considering the depth of the brushland and the blindness of its cover. But in the press of time and because he had not thought ahead to the complication of Chivo picking up more arms en route, Shonto had not taken the precaution he ordinarily would have of gagging the captive colonel.

He thought of it, now, as Ortega's galling shout echoed down the slope they were climbing.

"*¡Aquí, aquí, muchachos!* I am here! I am here!"

His head was hanging on the side of the horse nearest Shonto. The shout for help was cut off by the toe of the gunman's boot knocking out four front teeth and knocking out, too, the owner of the teeth. But the price of poker had just gone up, regardless.

"Chamaco," he said, "we have one chance: to split up."

"Never, patrón."

"Listen, kid"—Shonto's voice went hard as quartz—"you do what I tell you. I'm running this show."

"No, my American friend, you are not." The denial did not come from the boy but from the small man in the black suit. "It is I who must say what will be. And I say we stay together. You are not with Spaniards, my friend. You are not with traitors who call themselves Mexicans. You are with Indians. Lead on, boy."

Shonto knew he was helpless. He knew, as well, that they were helpless, that it would be but a matter of minutes before the *rurales* would come up to them, blind brush or not. They were so close behind that they could follow by ear the sounds of the stagecoach horses breaking through the brush. The rifle firing would commence any moment, and a bullet, unaimed except by the noise of their ponies crashing ahead, would soon enough find all and each of them. There was no other end within reason.

Yet Chamaco Díaz was no victim of such knowledge.

He had been supported by his Presidente, had heard him with his own ears say, "You are with Indians." What was not possible in the service of such a man?

"¡Patrón!" he now called to Shonto, voice high and

sharp with excitement. "There is a way. Follow me, and don't worry about making noise. The Rangers from your *Tejas* side of the river did not always obey the law!"

Their horses were plowing on up the slope now, and true to Shonto's fear the guerrillas were beginning to fire blindly at the sounds of their progress. The bullets hissed and sung about them. But the boy's shout had intrigued Charlie Shonto.

"What's that?" he yelled back.

"The Rangers of Texas," answered the boy, laughing for the first time in Shontro's memory of him. "Many times they would run the Apaches right on across the river, patrón. Then the Apaches had to have a way on this side to 'lose' them. I know the way, patrón. Ride hard and jump your horse when I demand it."

Shonto wanted to know more about that "jump" business, but the guerrillas were too close now. All he could do was bend low in the saddle and hope the bullet with his name on it went astray. It did. They came to Chamaco's "jumping place" without a wound. The place itself was a declivity in the trial—dug by hand and centuries gone—where no rider, not knowing that it waited beyond the steeply descending hairpin turn which hid it from above, could ever lift his mount over it in time. The animal's momentum, coming down the roof-steep pitch of the decline, would have to carry it and its rider into the "Ranger trap." And this is the way that it worked with the eager *rurales* of Chivo. All of the horses of Chamaco's party, even the pack horse with Colonel Ortega's unconscious form, cleared the break in the trail, leaping it like deer because spurred to the effort by their desperate riders. But the mounts of the guerrillas, scrambling around the hairpin, snorting furiously under the urging of their savage masters—the scent of the kill hot in the nostrils now, so close were they—had no chance to see or to lift themselves and their riders over the yawning pit. Into the waiting blackness of the man-made chasm the first dozen horses and soldiers went screaming and kicking. Another dozen soldiers and their mounts piled up in the trail above and did not plunge into the abyss with the others. But neither did they seem to retain their previous eagerness for the blood of El Presidente and the elevation of Lieutenant Chivo to the rank of Executioner of Camargo.

As for Chivo, himself, Shonto never knew if he was among the first group of riders, or the second. All that he did know was that, following the first terrible spate of screamings from the fallen, he did not hear again the harsh yelping voice of the bearded lieutenant.

"*¡Madre!* Chamaco," he said to the Indian boy, in the first moment of stillness following the piteous cries from above, "what is in that Apache trench up there?"

"Tiger's teeth," said the youth, "their points burned to hardness of iron, their butts set in the cracks of the mother rock. I don't wonder at the screams, patrón. I've looked down in that hole."

"*¡Santísima!*" breathed Shonto. "A staked pit!"

"For a pack of animals, the death of a pack of animals." The Oaxacan accents of El Presidente seemed sad. "Let us go on and catch that train in Toltepec. There is so much work to do in Mexico. The people cry out to me, and there is little time, so little time, for me to answer them."

Shonto did not answer, feeling the moment belonged to another. Chamaco understood the courtesy.

"Yes, Presidente," he said softly. "Please to follow your humble servant."

At once the small man in the black suit spurred his horse up beside that of the Chihuahua Indian boy.

"You are no one's humble servant," he said sternly. "Remember that always. You are a citizen of Mexico, a free man, humble to no one. If you believe in a god, you can thank him for that. If you believe in a man, you can thank a man."

"Yes, Presidente, I thank you *and* God."

"In that order, eh, boy?" A trace of warm amusement crossed the dark Indian features. "But you are wrong about the man, *muchacho*. It is another Presidente whom I charge you to remember. See that you don't forget his name, citizen; you owe it your life. Burn it in your mind, if you are a true Mexican: *Abraham Lincoln.*"

It was all downhill from there. Some minutes short of

midnight, Shonto rode into Toltepec with his charges. By a quarter past the hour, "Item Thirteen" was aboard the waiting train. Steam being up and the dawn all too near, the parting was abrupt. Camargo must be run past in the dark. Also, for the benefit of good health, those who must remain behind when the train pulled out would do well to be drawing in American air come sunrise of that risky day. El Presidente, surrounded by his faithful guard aboard the train, was virtually "taken away" from Shonto and Chamaco. So, as well, was the one-time Executioner of Camargo. In a last-second view, El Presidente seemed to spy the tall American and the tiny Indian boy sitting their horses in the lamplight spilling from his car's window. Shonto and Chamaco thought they saw him wave to them, and they returned the wave, each with his own thoughts. If the Texas gunman saw the bright tears streaming down the dark cheeks of Chamaco Díaz, he said nothing of the matter, then or later. Each man was permitted his own manner of farewell. But when the train had pulled away from Toltepec—before, even, its smoke had trailed into the Chihuahua night behind it—Charlie Shonto knew all he ever cared to know of the ending of the story. His big hand reached through the dark to touch the knee of his companion.

"Come along, Chamaco," he said. "We had better make long tracks. It's forty-nine miles to the river."

The boy nodded obediently, saying nothing. They turned their horses and sent them into a weary lope.

As they rode, Shonto's rawhide features softened. He was watching the proud set of the thin figure riding by his side. He was aware, surely, that the small Indian man in the ill-fitting black suit had been Benito Juárez, the liberator of Mexico, his people's Abraham Lincoln. But that part of it did not impress the big gunman unduly. For Charlie Shonto, the biggest Indian that he saw that night was always a little Chihuahua boy who barely reached to his gunbelt. History would not record, Shonto suspected, the secret fact that Juárez had been spirited to the Capitol in Washington, D.C. History would never record, he knew certainly, the added fact of the strange manner in which the legendary El Indio had been returned safely to his native land. But Charlie Shonto and Texas Express would know the way that it was done, and so would the tallest Indian in all of Toltepec!

When he thought of that, somehow even Charlie Shonto felt better. When the shadows of the Toltepec hills closed behind them, he was sitting as straight in the saddle as Chamaco Díaz.

But of course not as tall.